Jane's Aliens

A Novel

Dianne Zimmermann

ISBN 978-1-943650-25-5

Published 2016 by BookCrafters, Parker, Colorado.
BookCrafters@comcast.net

Copies of this book may be ordered from
www.bookcrafters.net
and other online bookstores.

*I dedicate this book to my friends
whose never-ending encouragement
drove me on when the going got tough.*

Acknowledgements

I would like to thank LA Mott
for reading, editing, and offering suggestions
and words of encouragement.

Chapter One

JANE CLARK, DEPUTY SHERIFF OF HANK COUNTY, Missouri had protected and served her county for over thirty years. Her first day was June 13, 1980. At that time, it was not easy trying to assimilate into a so-called "man's" job in a conservative county. Although Lynden Johnson issued an executive order for Affirmation Action Bill 1967 requiring employers to hire minority groups, men did not want women on the job. Jane remembered that most of the men accepted her, but a few were rude and crude, always playing jokes; setting her up with what they called practical jokes such as breaking into her work locker and hiding her personal belongings. Her fellow egotistical co-deputies even went so far as to let the air out of her patrol car tires. Captain Mike put a stop to their pranks saying they would be ousted out of the department if they continued their pranks. Jane was always the classy one, and careful, not to get mad or report those fellow officers who tried to make a fool of her. She merely rode it out until they became bored by not getting a reaction from her.

The men in her division learned to respect her after she covered for them in a few tough situations. She could hold her own, proving her physical and mental talents when she single-handedly stopped an attempted service station holdup by tackling an armed perpetrator. She surprised him by coming up the snack isle and slipping her arm around his outstretched arm, twisting it, coming down around and flipping the six foot plus man over her back onto the floor. She then disarmed and hand cuffed the man. The store attendant was astonished and bragged about her all over town. From that day forward she was looked upon with great respect. Fellow officers would no longer make sexist remarks towards her. They respected her, and the male dominated culture of the old days ended with her help. Men learned to respect women and women learned that they were capable of doing so much more if they had the desire and got proper training. Some of the women and girls in town wanted to learn judo and personal safety training from Jane, so she agreed to hold some classes in the school gym after school for anyone who wanted to learn.

Jane enjoyed being a deputy sheriff. She felt authoritative in her uniform and people respected her out of uniform too. Jane practically knew everyone in the county. It was a peaceful quiet county for the most part and Jane could count the number of times during her thirty-year career when she had to actually put someone in jail. She had gained lots of respect through the years; so much, that when teenagers would act up their mother's would threaten "don't make me call Deputy Jane on you." The kids would laugh, but they knew to straighten up, behave, and stop fighting amongst themselves. It worked for a while anyway, until the threat wore off, or mischievous teenage hormones raged. Jane learned to become more creative through the years, and would threaten to call the Aliens on the teenagers. She often got the kids thinking, although they knew she was teasing them most of the time. Jane would tell them that she knew some Aliens and they had agreed to help straighten bad kids out. The kids would laugh, but they were never sure if deputy Jane was joking or not. She got their creative juices flowing and their curiosity heightened anyway. Many of the teenagers got together and formed a star gazing and Alien search club. They would gather at night in the empty fields by one of their houses, and lay back on lounge chairs staring at the night sky, and wait for the Aliens to show up. She raised their curiosity and the kids stayed off the street. Several even claimed to had seen silver circular ships flash across the night sky. Jane had won their respect. It wasn't that Jane was big and tall with a threatening appearance; rather, it was just the opposite. Jane was a little taller than average height. She had long legs, a slender athletic figure and a sweet disposition. It was her sweet disposition that won everyone over. People would say she was just so nice, when she pulled you over for speeding, that she made you feel bad and you wanted to stay within the speed limit. She made you feel guilty and you wanted to cry because she actually cared about you getting home safely. Drivers that she had pulled over, would say that If you felt like no one cared about you, if you just had one of those days when nothing went right; well, after Jane pulled you over you just felt bad but you felt like somebody cared about you. Jane even made the would be drunk drivers feel bad. So they left their cars parked at the bars. They would walk or have someone come get them as not to disappoint Deputy Jane. She didn't have to ticket or arrest people very often.

Chapter Two

Jane spent her days and nights cruising the highways and county roads. She checked on abandoned properties, seems that there were more and more cases of foreclosures since the housing bubble crash in 2008. When Wall Street was too big to fail and taxpayers bailed them out. They got richer and the taxpayer got poorer as they slipped further and further from middle class into a working poor class. A class where wages were stagnant and did not keep up with the cost of living. Another thing that was getting Jane down, was all the talk about engineered foods containing toxic pesticides and herbicides. The food was no good for people and eventually made them sick; this of course, made huge profits for medical industry billionaires as they sold their pills, chemo treatments and radiation. Jane's wish was that one day people would rise up and get a fair shake and that the government would outlaw the bribing of elected officials by large corporations. Jane was passionate about wanting to see justice for the taxpayers. It seemed to Jane that the less she read the newspaper and listened to the news, the less she became upset with the current status quo of power gripping greed in the country. It benefited Jane's state of mind not to listen to the news or to watch her favorite channel, the NEWS cable station. All the negativity got her down in the dumps. Jane figured she just needed some spice in her life and to stop thinking about all this drudgery. So one day she asked the universe to send her some fun, and some love, which she had not had, since long before she divorced her husband George. It was time to dream a new love into her life.

Jane believed that thoughts were very powerful and that people could think their realities into being. She knew she was intuitively connected with the universe so she put her request out there. She went to bed after an exhausting eighteen hours of working overtime. She was out like a light in seconds, and fell into a very deep trance-like sleep and dreamed of falling in love.

****

It was the spry young red rooster that she had added to her flock of chickens that woke her up. Apparently It had learned how to crow just that morning. And his continuous joy in discovering his own voice woke her up out of a sound sleep.

It was daybreak, a beautiful warm sunny early autumn day by the time Jane was out patrolling the county roads

She had just checked out the Taylor's abandoned farm place and was heading down their dusty rocky lane when she spotted a speeding vehicle fast approaching down the highway. After the speeding car whizzed by, just barely missing the mailbox at the end of the lane, Jane pulled out and followed in hot pursuit. She had to step on it to catch up with the speeding car. She turned on her flashing lights. Her heart pounded as the speedometer approached near ninety miles per hour. The light blue Chevy was unfamiliar to her and boy was it zipping along, Jane exceeded speeds of ninety-five miles per hour just to catch up to it. It was only after Jane hit the siren did the speeding car finally slow down enough to pull over to the shoulder of the highway. Jane pulled over right behind the dusty car, which appeared to be several years old. It was obvious someone kept it up and in good condition, and Jane noted that the tags and plates were up to date.

Jane found herself shaking just a bit as she grabbed her uniform hat and put it on her head, checked her revolver in her holster and got out of her patrol car to walk toward the car. The driver lowered her window, then sat with her hands resting on the steering wheel. She was ready with driver's license in one hand and proof of insurance in the other hand. Jane approached the car window, carefully lifting the brim of her hat as she slightly bent at the waist in order to get a better look at the driver. Jane had never seen this attractive woman in the area before, she knew that she would certainly have remembered if she had.

"Good morning officer," the driver had taken off her sunglasses and flashed lovely blue eyes looking deeply into Jane's. Jane felt a sudden lump in her throat as she got lost in the woman's eyes. Just who pulled over who, here? Jane was breathless and had to concentrate hard to appear professional.

"I am afraid that I might have been speeding a bit," the driver humbly admitted.

"Yes, you were, I clocked you doing eighty-six in a seventy mile per hour zone," Jane stated, and was surprised and pleased that the speeder admitted guilt; usually speeders argue with her or, state a laundry list of flimsy excuses. One of Jane's all-time favorite excuses was an elderly woman speeding to get to the gas station before running out of gas; that was a classic.

"Well, I guess I have no excuse," pleaded the driver, as if reading Jane's mind. She spoke in a soft tone that did not go unnoticed by Jane. In fact, Jane found herself infatuated by the driver, and her lovely blue eyes; eyes that peered deep into hers, making it hard to concentrate.

"Ah, registration and personal property tax receipt?" Jane managed to ask beginning to perspire under the heaviness of her uniform.

The blonde haired, blue-eyed driver leaned over, showing a bit of cleavage, as she reached to the right side of the car to open the glove compartment. She pushed the button to open the compartment and flipped through a few pieces of paper and envelopes, finally pulling out a hand full of insurance and registration documents and said she hoped she had the personal property papers in there somewhere too.

"This should be it," she said handing the mitt full of papers to Jane then straightening her blouse absentmindedly.

"I'll just take all of this," Jane said as she took hold of the papers before the wind blew them away. Gripping them in a fist lock with both hands, she walked back towards to her patrol car. Her official uniform boots crunching the small rocks on the shoulder of the road reminded her that she was in control, not the pretty blue-eyed blonde. Jane managed to open her patrol car door by shifting the papers to her left hand. She slid in behind the wheel, breathing in relief but not escaping the sky blue eyes now permanently etched in her mind's eye. She left out a deep sigh and searched through the documents all the while smelling sweet perfume that captivated her. Still, she managed in routine police fashion to complete the tasks at hand. She proceeded to check the validity of the woman's driver's license, license plates, insurance and registration information. It took her a few minutes, but with the computer mounted on the dashboard in her patrol car, she brought up all the information that she needed to check on the driver. There were no outstanding tickets or warrants. When she finished she walked back up to the woman's car to the driver side window handing the papers back to the driver.

"I'm going to give you a warning ticket today, Alice Manning. I see you are new to the area."

"Oh thank you," Alice said and added, "yes, I am new to the area." Alice smiled and tears pooled in her lovely blue eyes. Alice knew she shouldn't cry in front of the deputy, but she was feeling very stressed. Even as she sat there her mind wandered. Her life had changed very drastically in the last six months. Her husband, Joe, was an active healthy guy who exercised regularly, but he got sick suddenly and died leaving her all alone. It all happened so suddenly; she was still in shock. In her mind, she blamed that horrible plant where he worked as a chemist assistant. He was laid off from his old job in the petroleum refinery and after a month of not finding work, he came across an ad in the paper. He went for an interview and accepted the job. Within a few weeks after he was hired, he was transferred to a plant in South Dakota. They had to move from Springfield, Illinois to a small town in South Dakota where Alice worked as a waitress in a small restaurant. The pay was good but she was sick of being propositioned all the time by male customers who worked the nearby natural gas field. Alice's wandering mind was pulled back into reality as she heard the deputy's voice at her car window.

"Be careful now and make it home safely," Deputy Jane cautioned and then added, "oh, and don't pick up any hitchhikers. I just got a report that a prisoner escaped from the state penitentiary this morning and could be in this area," warned Jane.

"Oh I will be careful, thank you officer," smiled Alice, tears still standing in her eyes.

Jane had seen that the woman was new to Hank, Missouri and recognized her address as being on Main Street. One thing for sure, the woman moved her. She never felt this way while looking into George's eyes, never, and she did not want to leave this moment behind and so she asked the driver a question.

"Is everything okay, you look a bit upset, is there anything wrong?" Jane asked, she had noticed the tears in the driver's eyes. It looked as if she had been upset and weary for some time.

"Oh, I moved to Hank to begin a new life after my husband died," Alice responded, her eyes tearing up. She struggled to continue, "He got sick not long after we moved up to South Dakota for his work, from Springfield, Illinois. I hated South Dakota, so did he, but the company he worked for paid him very well. We didn't get along. I thought about leaving him, but then he got sick, and the plant transferred him back to Springfield, Illinois. There I went to cosmetology school, while Joe worked part time; that is, until he got too sick to work. After he died, I needed a new start and somehow ended up in Hank."

"Well, I am so sorry to hear about your tough times." Jane felt sorry for the woman as she handed her the yellow warning slip through the open window then patted the window sill in a gesture of sympathy.

"You just be careful now and take it easy," Jane said. Then she walked back to her patrol car, got in, and watched the woman pull away. A part of Jane's heart drove off in that car along with that lovely woman.

There was just something about her sad eyes that touched Jane's heart. Jane could not get the blue eyed lovely Alice out of her mind.

Chapter Three

Jane went about her duties that day answering calls about break ins and reported accidents, and abandoned cars. The department was on high alert because of the recent escaped prisoner. Jane was extra cautious when she drove back to her farm that evening after work. She looked around the farm yard and out buildings for anything unusual. Then she walked up to the porch and unlocked the door, looked in her house, turned on the lights then walked through the house looking in every room and behind the doors. Her house wasn't that big, just a modest two bedrooms, one bath with a small living room and kitchen. When she felt that everything was in order, she changed out of her uniform and into her faded jeans and t-shirt to go out and feed her animals and make sure that they were all secure for the night. She had four goats in the barn and a henhouse and fenced pen filled with chickens. As she went about filling up feeders and pouring water into water pans she counted her blessings. She was healthy and fortunate enough to make a comfortable living patrolling a fairly peaceful community. She was lonely at times but grateful for her quiet life without negative George. She was grateful that her divorce from George was not contested. Although George said that he was angry about the divorce Jane thought it was more of an act. She was a cop after all and had done a little investigating and learned that he had had a girlfriend on the side for months. Jane figured he intentionally aggravated her so she would want to divorce him and set him free to marry the young girl that he was dating.

After Jane finished her chores, she made sure that she secured the gate and headed back to the house. When she got inside she looked behind each door and rechecked every room. She then settled in to reheat the leftover spaghetti and meatballs she had cooked the night before. She toasted garlic bread, made salad from fresh fixings straight from the garden. She filled her plate and poured herself a glass of wine. As she ate her dinner, she read the Hank weekly paper. She looked it over carefully. She had edited this edition. It was her job to substitute for the regular editor from time to time. She was disappointed when she noticed an article that had spelling and grammar mistakes. She made a mental note to double check her work next time.

The house felt disturbingly silent, as Jane sat at the kitchen table feeling lonely. A mystic vision of the blue-eyed woman she met earlier in the day, weaved in and out of her heart's mind as she went through the motions of eating her dinner. There was an eerie feeling in the air, as if the dull silence of solitude was about to be abruptly disturbed. She didn't have to wait long for in a nanosecond, she was jarred back from her daydreaming into a frightening reality. The kitchen door burst open and banged against the wall, rattling the kitchen windows. She jumped in her chair and nearly knocked over the glass of wine. At first she thought it was a burst of wind that flung open an unlatched door. Then she saw it, a figure standing in the doorway. She wished it had been the wind, when she realized a shadow of a man stood staring at her. Jane cursed herself for forgetting to lock the door. She jumped from her seat and reached at her waistband for her service revolver which was not there. The tall male figure took several steps into the room then stood under the ceiling light near the table. Jane saw a tall, skinny, dirty faced man with a fresh prison buzz cut. He was waving a gun at her. He looked angry and when he spoke, his voice was low but deep and shaky. She had to strain to hear him, he spoke barely above an angry whisper.

"Don't move!" the man demanded. He pointed the gun at her and scanned the room at the same time, his eyes moving from side to side taking every inch in. He searched for anyone else who could have been there with her. Then he spotted the all too familiar shirt. It was then he realized where he was standing in the home of a deputy sheriff.

"Oh crap, a cop," the man grunted after looking at her

and then turning slightly saw an all too recognizable tan colored county sheriff uniform shirt that was hanging on a hanger on the bedroom door off from the kitchen. He looked at her, then back at the uniform shirt, deciding if the size of the shirt matched her size, or was there a man too somewhere in the house.

"Yours?" the anxious man demanded as he pointed with his gun at the uniform shirt.

"Oh, yeah," Jane said as she sat with her hands placed on the table in front of her. He then walked around the table so he could look at her dead on.

"You the guy who escaped?" Jane asked trying to sound authoritative.

"Maybe. You here alone?" the intruder asked and expected her to nod yes, and she did.

Seems they just stared at each other for a few moments, neither knowing what to say to the other. The escapee knew that as soon as he would leave the house, she would make a call and the cops would be swarming after him. He did not want to stay there. He could kill her, he thought, since he was in jail for murder anyway. But he did not want to kill her; she had done nothing to him. Oh, he killed his crooked business partner, shot him point blank, but he deserved it. He deserved it for cheating him out of millions. The bastard added insult to injury by having an affair with his wife. In one sickening swoop his life changed forever. He had lost his business, his best friend, his wife, his home and his freedom. That man deserved to die. It was justifiable homicide in the first degree. But now, with this woman sitting in front of him looking at him in a curious way, he just didn't quite know what to do. He had nothing against her only that she was there; but, still she had done nothing to him. Thoughts raced through his mind. Then she spoke in a low steady unthreatening tone.

"What's your name?" Jane had asked. She gently motioned for him to sit on the chair across from her at the table. He remained oddly calm, as if too tired to think about what to do next. Jane made sure as she sat there that her hands remained visible on the table in front of her. She saw he looked with hungry eyes at the empty plate in front of her.

"The name is Steve." Not ready to share his last name out of fear or shame, he added, "I am sure that you have heard about me by now."

"Yes, I have," Jane responded cautiously, being careful not to make any sudden moves. She sat watching him. She almost felt sorry for him and offered him some food as he sat down across from her at the kitchen table.

"How about I fix you a plate of spaghetti or a sandwich? You can take my old truck that is out there in the barn and be on your way. I don't want trouble," Jane said, in a calm voice, and then continued, "Hey, I am about to retire and I would like to live out an enjoyable retirement." She was not about to beg but she was serious. She was all too willing to bargain for her life at this stage of the game. Jane was getting a feel for the guy sitting across from her now. He was tired she could tell. His breathing became more regular now, as if he was calming down a bit. He was scared, she could sense it.

She could sense too, that he wasn't an evil man, down deep, and that someone had done him wrong and in a knee-jerk moment he reacted unwisely. She had a special intuitive gift when it came to human behavior, especially if they were frightened. This intuition had served her very well through the years as she dealt with criminals.

Jane could read people's psychic, a talent that was, at times, troublesome to her. She found that knowing why people were the way they were, or why they did the things they did was annoying at times. She did not want to know what made people tick. But, it was as if the negativity clung to her clothes and to the air that she breathed in. Jane was intuitive, psychic, had a sense about this frightened man. Why should either one of them die, she thought. She couldn't believe what she was thinking and feeling. Somehow upholding the law in every situation just didn't seem so important anymore. He shared with her what had happened and why he was in prison. Her intuition had been right on point. The people closest to him had done him wrong. He had been in a rage and was not thinking straight. It was clearly a crime of passion. Jane wondered if she was really psychic or just in law enforcement long enough where you get to the point that you can read the looks on people's faces and know just what went on with them.

"I can heat up some spaghetti or make sandwiches for you, how would that be?" she repeated her earlier offer.

"Okay, get up and make me a couple of sandwiches,"

he ordered by making a pointing motion with his gun towards the refrigerator. He turned ever so slightly then in the chair so he could keep an eye on her. Jane thought that he was trying very hard to sound more threatening then she felt that he was; to her, he was an emotionally tormented soul. Jane saw that he was weak with hunger and fatigue and for a moment thought about overpowering him, then thought better of it. She had to remind herself, that It was too close to retirement. Again, with a brisk arm movement he motioned with the gun as if to say, hurry up.

"Don't try anything stupid," he said as if he could read her thoughts. She had glanced at the gun while getting up from her chair. Jane could see him quickly eyeing her service revolver that laid on the top of the bureau. Jane quickly abandoned the many years of reflex training of rushing for her gun, instead she took a couple of steps towards the refrigerator. She got the package of sliced ham, jars of pickles and mustard out of the refrigerator and placed them on the kitchen counter. She slowly and cautiously reached up and opened the cupboard door above her head and retrieved the loaf of bread and got a table knife out of the drawer. She began making sandwiches as he closely watched her. She made sure that she kept slightly turned so he could see what she was doing. He watched her every move. She was cautious but not frightened. She sensed he was more frightened than her. Her plan was not to make him mad and to get him out of her house as fast as she could persuade him to leave.

"Where are the keys to the truck I saw was in the barn? Is there gas in it?" He was agitated and sweating profusely. His hair, forehead and shirt wet with sweat. Jane thought he must be frightened out of his wits. For a moment she thought again about rushing him and tackling him to the floor. She then thought better of it, for what if something went wrong and the gun went off? Jane had to push back her police training and think of her upcoming retirement and possibly a new life with Alice.

"I'll give you a head start," Jane finally said slowly, "before I call it in. I'll say I left my keys in the truck in the barn and when I happened to look out the window, noticed that it was gone."

"I appreciate that," the shaking man replied in a low tone as if too tired and hungry to speak.

Jane knew that the man would not get far. She knew that he knew the cops would kill him on the spot if they found out that he killed a fellow officer. Besides she had a gun pointed at her and this was no time in her life to be a hero. Perhaps she just got more frightened the older she got, or smarter, who's to say. But as the minutes passed, she was becoming more convinced that it was time to retire. She only prayed that this man would not go berserk and kill her. It seemed he relaxed a bit then as if he trusted her somehow and began to talk to her.

"I just had to break out of that prison. I couldn't stand another day all penned up," the man said appearing to begin to cry, but suddenly bringing himself back to the reality at hand.

"Why did I have to pick this house?" The man sounded disgusted with himself and then desperate "but I was hungry and thirsty."

Jane filled a glass of water and set it on the table. He looked at her, studied her wondering if he could trust her. He hesitated, but desperate thirst won out, and he carefully picked up the glass with a steady left hand while continually holding the gun in his right. He asked for another, she obliged him getting it out of the faucet at the sink. She then went back to making the sandwiches. He ate two, while she made two more, wrapping them and placing them in a paper lunch bag. She hoped somehow the gesture dredged up maternal childhood feelings. She thought it did by the brief sad look in his eyes when he took the bag from her.

"I put two bottles of water in this bag for you. How about a couple of apples?" Jane added almost feeling like a mother for a weird moment. He felt it too, her motherly nature.

Perhaps he became afraid then and could not trust what he was feeling and as Jane turned slightly to get a couple of apples out of the bowl on the counter, she felt a sudden sharp blow to the back of her head and fell unconscious to the floor. He had panicked and hit her hard with his gun. He hated to do it but he could take no chances, he needed a huge head start. She appeared to be alive when he turned and looked back at her, as he headed out the door with the bag of sandwiches and water bottles. He felt guilty for hitting her, but it was done now. She moved ever so slightly, so he knew she was still alive. He was glad she was alive because at first he thought he hit her too hard. He did not want to kill her he only wanted a head start. He needed the extra time that knocking her unconscious brought him, otherwise he knew that she would be on the phone calling the cops. He just could not leave her sitting there. Besides she would have felt compelled as a deputy to try to stop him. Guess, he thought, that he could have gagged her and tied her up; oh well, too late for that. Besides, he didn't have anything to tie her up with. It wasn't like he had time to search for rope. It's done, he thought, and he was out the door.

The escapee stumbled down the porch steps and nearly fell trying to find his way in the dim light. Quickly he made his way in the dark across the yard to the barn. When he got inside the barn he was pleased to see that the truck, although old and beatup did look drivable. He quickly looked into the driver side window where he saw the keys dangling from the ignition switch. The keys were there just like she said, and that made him feel even more guilty for hitting her. He did not have time to feel bad for long. It was time to move and he was in a hurry. He saw the doors were unlocked and quickly climbed into the old truck. The paint was faded, it was rusted in spots, the cracked leather seats were torn in places. He held his breath as he turned the key then let out a sigh when the motor started right up. She did not lie. And the gas gauge showed a full gas tank like she had said. A feeling of guilt for hitting her crept under his skin again, he shook it off. He didn't have time for sentiment, he had to get going. He slowly pushed in the clutch in with is left foot and moved the floor shifter into reverse. The transmission made a horrible grinding sound as the gear engaged when he slowly let out the clutch. He was grateful that he had learned to drive a standard shift as a kid while he worked at his dad's garden and landscaping business. Looking in the rearview mirror, he slowly backed the old truck out of the barn, turning slightly to face the driveway leading away from the farm place. He shifted the old truck into first gear, chugged pass the house, then gave it more gas and shifted into second as he headed down the lane into the night smiling. Bouncing down the rutted road, steering with his left hand, with his right, feeling into the brown paper bag he reached in and pulled out a sandwich. He was nervous and eating helped just has it always had when he and his best friend business partner, were nervous about taking over his dying dad's business. While looking straight ahead, he carefully unwrapped the wax paper from around the sandwich, being careful not to let the pickles slip out onto his lap. Watching the road, he took a bite. Busy watching where he was driving and eating at the same time, he did not notice the dim amber lights in the sky approaching overhead above him ever so silently. The craft hovered above the old faded red pickup that was roaring into third gear heading down the county road in the opposite direction of town. The three aliens inside the spacecraft were watching the escapee. They had plans for him.

Chapter Four

Jane, an alien hybrid, of which she was not aware, was assigned the three protective alien Watchers by her alien father. To borrow humankind's religious terms, they were her guardian angels. Religion hinted at extraterrestrial higher power by creating their own religious winged figures they called angels. And with the aid of government secrecy, turned any belief of extraterrestrials into a self-serving belief of their own creations. The church taught that there were angels, but said extraterrestrial beings from other planets were fictional. The three Watchers in the spacecraft that hovered above the old rusted pickup truck were good aliens. They were from the Pleiades seven sisters blue star constellation. These Watchers, the good aliens, were benevolent to planet Earth. They kept the Earth safe from bad alien beings who wanted to see Earth destroyed. These three were about to show themselves to the escapee.

A strange thing happened to Jane as she laid unconscious on the floor in her kitchen. She thought that she had died and crossed over to the spiritual side. She saw a bright light. The light beckoned her, calling her name.

"Whoever you are—turn off that light! You are blinding me!" Jane was confused and afraid. When the escapee hit her and as she fell to the floor, she had felt her spiritual being raise to the ceiling and beyond. From up high, she had looked down at her body. As she rose further into a bright light, she saw her childhood dog, Emma, happily wagging her tail. She saw her favorite Aunt Ally, who had passed years before. She heard her aunt speak to her from the other side.

"It's not time yet," her Aunt Ally said over and over again in an angelic voice. "Go back, go back!"

Jane wanted to stay there, on the other side, with her dog and Aunt Ally, but she felt herself slipping back into her physical body.

She woke up and found herself still lying in the same place on the kitchen floor. For a moment, she was sad for she hated to leave the warm light of her love ones in the spiritual plane. She realized that she had just been gifted with a visit to the other side.

Heaven, she thought. She had just visited heaven. It was the strangest, yet most beautiful thing, like a special gift. Jane felt sad that she could not stay there in the light for it felt like home, warm, loving and peaceful.

Did she die and come back? Did she have a near death experience? She wasn't sure what had happened. But, she was faced with another other worldly dilemma. Who or what were these alien creatures standing over her, looking down at her, as she laid on the floor.

"Am I dead?" She asked herself. She was afraid to try to get up off the floor because she felt dizzy when she raised her head even the slightest bit. Her hand found a huge lump on the back of her head than she remembered she was hit by the escapee. Her head ached from the blow, and now her eyes were blinded by a terrific glare. She had to use both hands to shield her eyes from the bright light.

"Jane, we are here to help you," one of the three spoke and she heard a small voice. What stood before her should have been more frightening then the escaped convict, at least he was human. These creatures looked unlike anything she had ever seen before except for in science fiction movies. The three who stood before her were indeed aliens? Did they come to her on Earth or had she landed on another planet?

"I must have gotten hit harder than what I thought," Jane said aloud to herself as she looked at the tiny figures all of about four feet tall standing before her.

"I must be smoking too much weed," she said aloud while she laid there on the floor rubbing the back of her aching head. Her breath caught in her throat as she heard a high-pitched tin sounding voice begin to speak.

"We like weed," one tiny figure said in a small mechanical voice. Jane did not know if she should be afraid, cry or bust out laughing. She chose a small smirk instead, that managed to get caught in her throat. She looked them over and for some strange reason, she immediately liked these small strange gray creatures with huge heads and large solid black almond shaped eyes, tiny holes for a nose and a small slit of a mouth.

"Jesus," was all Jane could say. She could not believe what was happening to her. First, she got knocked on the head, then saw passed love ones, and now she was seeing little aliens.

"I must have gotten hit harder than what I thought," Jane whispered to herself again. She could not believe what was happening.

"We want some weed," the slightly taller of the three alien creatures said. Jane was a hybrid. Of course, she did not know that she was a hybrid, but it was the reason why she immediately felt a fondness for these little guys. Unbeknownst to Jane, the aliens knew that one night her mother had been taken up into a space craft. Several of her eggs were harvested and inseminated by aliens. One fertilized egg was placed back into her mother's womb and nine months later Jane was born. Jane's mother and human father were unaware and thought Jane was all theirs. The three aliens had been assigned by the father alien to watch over Jane. They had guarded her all of her life and it was now time for Jane to meet her guardians. Jane would naturally not be afraid of them and they knew this so decided to have a little fun with her.

"Jesus," Jane whispered again, she knew she had just

died and returned. She was dumbfounded by what she was witnessing. One of the little figures began snooping around and opening cabinets looking into drawers and using a kitchen chair climbed up on the counter top so he could reach the cupboards and the canisters that were sitting there.

"Oh, weed!" He said as he twisted off the lid of the canister and pulled out the small cloth bag. He smelled the sweet fragrance that permeated from the bag. His little slit of a mouth curved into a smile. The canister was filled with marijuana buds along with a small pipe and lighter tucked in the canister alongside the bag of buds.

"How convenient," he said as he took them out and placed a bud into the pipe bowl and putting it to his tiny mouth, lit it, inhaled and held it in as long as he could. He coughed a bit, then laughed. He climbed down from the counter top with the pipe and lighter and sat on a kitchen chair. He sat sideways with one arm rested on the back of the chair and his little legs crossed at the knees. Sitting tall and sophisticated like, he stuck the tip of the pipe in his little slit of a mouth and inhaled, then smiled with pleasure.

"Jesus," Jane said aloud to herself, she could not believe what she was witnessing.

"We are not what you call 'Jesus' we are from the Pleiades, blue star seven sisters star cluster in the Orion belt, house of Taurus star cancellation, the Pleiades, I say. We are the Pleiadians, guardians of planet Earth." He rattled off in a mechanical voice as if the information was programmed within, then snickered, obviously feeling high.

"We have come here for weed," the tallest one said as he passed the pipe amongst his two companions and then passed the pipe to Jane who had rolled up to a sitting position and sat cross legged on the floor.

"Jesus," Jane sighed in disbelief as she sat crosslegged on the floor as the three aliens watched her; then, sat crosslegged on the floor with her. She got lost watching her reflection in their huge eyes. The weed was making her dizzy and high. She was surprised, that she was not afraid of them; rather, she felt an odd connection with them, somehow. They passed her the pipe and lighter and she readily took it, lit it and took a huge hit. She coughed a bit and said, "Jesus."

"Stop calling us Jesus," the one called Moe said in a squeaky voice as he took the pipe from Jane. He took a hit, then introduced each of his friends to Jane before he passed it on to the alien seated next to him, called Larry. Larry took a hit, then passed the pipe to the next alien in line, named Curly. Curly took the pipe and looked at it, as he sized it up, then pressed it to his small slit of a mouth. Taking a deep breath, he took a big hit, coughed a little sound of a cough, then smiled a little slit of a smile.

"Oh, good stuff Jane," and a slight curve gave way to a smile on his tiny mouth.

"Who? Ah, hell I'm not nuts, I know I am sharing weed with three aliens," Jane thought. She decided to ask them some questions, her head hurt, but the aliens being such a huge distraction, took her mind off of her pain and the throbbing bump on her head. All four of them sat crossed legged sitting on the floor in a circle. Jane so wanted to take out her smartphone, record the event, and take a Facebook picture but hesitated at the thought of them probably not wanting her to do that. Would they even show up on a picture, she wondered? Maybe no one was supposed to know that they were here in her kitchen. She decided to wait.

"Go ahead Jane take the picture," snickered Curly.

"Oh, oh, I know I did not say that out loud." Jane was taken back and suddenly realized they could read her mind.

"You got it Jane," smiled Larry taking another hit. "We like you Jane, you are one of us."

"What do you mean?" asked Jane "You're not suggesting that I am like you? I don't look like you?"

"No matter Jane, there are many hybrids on this planet Earth."

"Why?" Jane's eyes were big in disbelief; no wonder she wasn't afraid of them.

"Because we need to upgrade and advance humankind, because they are moving too slow in advancement, seems all the powerful know is greed and war," Moe explained, then went on.

"Humans are not advancing fast enough to be able to accept that we are here. They should be moving from hate and greed to love for all. Your leaders pretend to be in conflict with other leaders, they pretend to have the majority of people's welfare in their thoughts. They only pretend. And they hide us, only allowing hints of truths to be exposed, little by little by mostly silly coverups when UFO's are reported. In other words they are not coming straight out and telling people that we aliens do exist and that we visit Earth all the time. Your leaders are more or less allowing people to come to their own conclusions. Roswell did happen, in July of 1947, because two opposing nations of aliens were fighting and a spacecraft was shot down. Your leaders were afraid to tell people, especially after the Orson Wells radio broadcast that frightened so many humans several years earlier," explained Moe.

"You mean that there is more than one race of aliens in space and they do not get along, just like humans here on Earth do not get along?"

"Well, yes. There is good and bad of us like there is good and bad of humankind. Now you know why religious teachings talk of angels and the devils, the evil ones. Religious leaders turned alien stories into religious tales to suit their own manipulation and control of the masses," Larry further explained.

"So I get the feeling this weed is not the only reason you are here?" Jane asked. "And how did you know that I even had any weed?" Jane asked, then, thinking her weed was so fragrant that they could probably smell it from outer space.

"No, Jane, weed is not the only reason we are here, although we really like your weed," smiled Curley "but, we are here to enlighten you so that you can enlighten others."

She took another hit from the pipe, after the alien

sitting next to her handed it to her nodding. She nodded back to him. And then, suddenly remembering her sheriff duties, she mumbled that she had to report the escapee and truck thief. She waved the pipe about and took another hit as she lit it with the lighter. In a hazy moment she realized that she did not care about the escapee whether he got caught or not, or about her truck.

"Oh the hell with it," she said out loud, after taking another hit from the pipe. The marijuana smoke filled the room and she felt light headed. She felt so much better; her head no longer ached. She did not care about the escapee. Besides, every sheriff in the county knew her rusted out, faded red old truck and if she wasn't driving it whoever was would get pulled over.

"My truck!" Jane suddenly said aloud after thinking about what had just happened to her. Never mind the aliens she was seeing in front of her, she couldn't even comprehend them, much less the small round silver space ship that glowed parked under the yard light in her back yard.

"Weed? They came for weed? Cool!" Jane was pleasantly high now, the situation became funny, she had to laugh at the craziness of it all. It was definitely a situation that warranted smoking some weed. What the hell, she'll probably get her old truck back soon. And once again, as if knowing what she was thinking, the alien next to her updated her.

"Jane, your truck is back in the barn and that man who took it, is back in prison," the shorter alien called Larry reported.

"We took care of it," Larry smiled very proudly Jane thought.

"How?" Jane asked, as she wondered out loud, she loved being high. This was some good stuff she blatantly grew in her garden. Yeah, growing weed was her only vice, other than that, she was a law abiding sheriff deputy. Medical marijuana was legal; she knew that recreational marijuana would soon be legal also. Besides, she was only growing a wee bit for her own personal use. She wasn't selling it. She listened then to the aliens' explanation as to how they returned her truck.

"When the bad boy who took your truck saw us hover over him, as he was driving down the road," smiled Larry. "He suddenly turned around and brought the truck back, jumped out then ran down to the tracks, hopped the train and headed back to prison," smiled Larry, "so no need to worry."

"Tell me more," smiled Jane feeling relaxed. "I want to be enlightened."

"Just like we got here, we use our thoughts to guide the craft. Our thoughts are our realities, just as you humans used to do when you had twelve strands of DNA before the bad aliens created hybrids with two strands. But even at double helix, two strands, humans do create their own reality by their thoughts they just do not realize it. We do not need a craft to travel, but we use the flying saucer space craft to be seen because humans are conditioned to expect to see it. We find that humans relate best to the round circular style saucer, for some reason, probably because of your movies. So we present that to you when we come to visit, if we want you to see us, that is. Otherwise we are here and everywhere, you just cannot see us. We are everywhere. We are like your religious Jesus, omnipresent. Your Earth's religion hinted at this when they created your god who they said was everywhere. The ancient humans were derived from aliens. Then they created their own god for their own use and that was to control mankind through teaching of sins, commandments and penance. You may think we are past souls who have lived on this planet in the physical, and some of us are, but some of us have only lived in the blue star cluster of the Pleiades. We are here to protect your planet from the greedy aliens who are part of the super capitalist destroyers of the planet."

It took all three of the aliens to explain this to Jane. They politely took turns speaking to her as she sat listening intently without interrupting them. She got their message even though she was high and in the zone.

"Pass the pipe please," Jane woozily said as she carefully got up from the floor and walked over and looked out the kitchen window above the sink. Sure enough, like the aliens said, by the glow from the yard light, she could see her truck was back in the barn, just like it was before the escapee took it. She guessed he took it. She did not know much about anything anymore, nor cared, as the weed was a relief and the effects soothed her. She was even beginning to feel comfortable around these little guys with big heads, big dark almond shaped eyes, that never blinked, small slit of a mouth, no ears, that she could see, and slender legs. Their feet and hands had three long digits. She felt weak suddenly, her head hurt badly. She wanted to pass out again but fought it off because she was more curious than shaken by these strange visitors.

"Just how many are there of you here and what are your real names?" Jane asked as she moved from the kitchen window over to the kitchen table to sit on a chair. She felt the knot on the back of her head again with her hand. At least, she had proof of being hit on the head otherwise she would have thought that she had gone totally crazy.

"I am Moe, this is Larry and he is Curly and that is all you need to know, sister." Moe said and smiled.

"Jesus!" Jane sighed, "Alien jokesters." She couldn't believe what she was hearing.

"We have no Jesus among us," Moe said as he refilled Jane's pipe with more of her weed from the little bag they had found in the counter top canister.

"Evidently you cannot grow weed where you come from Moe, Larry and Curly," Jane mocked.

"Oh yes, we can. We just have to think it and it is there."

"What? Jesus!"

"It's Moe, Larry and Curly, not What or Jesus," chided the one called Larry, impatiently.

"I must be out of my head," Jane muttered then taking her hand to her head to make sure the bump was there. Something had to cause this crazy illusion she was experiencing.

"You are not out of your head, you are high." Curly smiled, "This is good stuff, we like your weed."

"We want you to grow lots of it," requested Moe. "We will guard the growth of it for you."

"I thought you could grow it with your minds?"

"We can, but we need to do it your way, while we are here," explained Larry.

"But be careful Jane, don't get caught, because it is illegal, still," Larry continued.

"I know," smirked Jane, "I'm a county sheriff deputy remember?" And then she had to laugh at the humor of it all. Actually, she thought that her head was feeling much better because she was smoking the fine weed that she grew.

"Jane be glad it is still illegal, even for a deputy sheriff, " Larry snickered.

"Because if it ever became legal and the tobacco companies or other big drug corporations got a hold of growing weed, you know they would add toxic additives and as a result of the toxicity, illness would abound," interjected Curly, "so just be careful."

"While you are here? How long are you going to be here?" asked Jane.

"We are your guardians Jane, you are part of us and your job is to expose the truth about many things," Moe informed Jane, who began to look very weary.

"I need to take a nap," and Jane walked over to the couch and laid down.

"We come back later, Jane" smiled Curly "have a nice nap. Not to worry. We shall return."

"Jesus..." and Jane fell asleep or passed out; or whatever. She didn't care. She heard the faint familiar, "We not Jesus," but, actually they were her Jesus and her guardian angels; especially if it was true that religious teachings covered up the fact of alien beings, and created god in their own human likeness, in order to manipulate and control people. But, at the moment she did not care, she needed sleep.

And then as quickly as they appeared, they disappeared. The aliens got into their spacecraft and vanished in a flash. They had more messages for Jane which they would deliver at a later time, it was best to let her rest now.

****

Jane slept through the night on the couch. When she awoke she thought that she had had the strangest dreams while she slept. In her dream an escaped prisoner busted into the back door of her house, knocked her on the head and took her truck, a frightening incident only to be followed by three amigo aliens who smoked her stash of weed. But it was not a dream. Her head hurt, her neck ached from sleeping with her head cocked crooked on the couch arm all night. She needed coffee bad but her coffee canister was empty. She quickly took a shower, got into her uniform and drove into town.

When Jane got to work she was surprised to learn that the escape convict everyone was searching for, had returned to prison on his own. Cable station, NEWS, reports stated that the convict appeared half crazed and scared out of his wits, and happy to be back. The NEWS video taken from prison security cameras showed that he knocked feverishly on the prison guard door, yelling for someone to let him in. He demanded they take him directly to his cell and make sure they secured the lock on the steel door.

Jane left the sheriff office and crossed the street to the coffee shop to visit with the customers there, in an attempt to create some sense of normalcy to her life, which of late just felt crazy. She knew she got hit on the head because the bump was still there, the aliens were there or was she just going crazy?

She got her coffee and pastry then turned to leave the coffee shop and practically ran head on into a lovely blonde headed woman. It was the woman named Alice, that she had pulled over for speeding earlier in the week, and now here she was smiling at her, those blue eyes peering directly into hers. Jane's heart pounded in her chest.

"Good morning," she managed to say as she was trying to catch her breath.

"Sheriff Jane, you'll be glad to know that I have been behaving," the lovely blonde said. Jane's heart jumped, she thought her whole world was out of whack ever since she pulled this woman over for speeding.

"I'm glad to hear that," smiled Jane, taking a step to

the side so Alice could pass by her. Alice had a handful of flyers that she was planning on placing on the bulletin board in the tiny coffee shop. She handed Jane a flyer which stated that Alice was offering fifty percent off of haircuts and other services for the next two weeks.

"Oh now that sounds like a good deal," Jane commented, "and I could use a trim."

"Great, please come in and see me," she said then moved on looking over her shoulder at Jane, and smiling. Then she added, "I'd love to see you again without having to break the law to do so." Alice smiled and winked, "I love a woman in uniform."

All Jane could do was stare after her, her heart fluttered. For ten whole seconds Jane could not move. "Jesus," she finally managed to say, "Jesus," Jane could only say in a low voice to herself as she walked across the street.

"What the…" She looked up and could see three small slender figures in the sheriff department office window. She gasped and hoped that she was the only one who saw them waving from the window. She looked up and down the street as she crossed it and it appeared people walking on the sidewalk near her office where too busy either on their way to their jobs, or towards the nearby grocery and hardware stores and did not see them.

"Did you call?" They asked in unison has she opened the sheriff office door. She was only too glad that fellow officers and the captain were out of the office on their rounds already.

"What are you doing here?" Jane asked them. Shocked to see them, in her office of all places.

"Didn't you call us?" The tallest of the three asked, "You called 'Jesus' did you not?"

"Jesus," Jane said out of frustration.

"We answer to "Jesus" because your small group of elite leaders created this Jesus and all humankind believe in him, but in essence this so called Jesus is from the Pleiades; we are your Jesus. Your elitist leaders want you to think that you are weak and need a god, a Jesus when you all are derived from aliens, like us. We are far more advanced than your leaders and they do not want you to know about us. They created this Jesus God you all pray to, because you were taught to believe that you are all weak sinners, when truth be told, your thoughts are very powerful. Your thoughts create your realities." Curly said, then realized that he had gone into a bit of a rant, and stood silent then.

"Jesus," Jane said again without realizing what she was saying.

"Yes," was said in union by the three.

"Well, I won't make that mistake again!"

"Jane, you do not need us now, but you will soon, and we are here to help you with a very important issue that is soon to develop."

"What?" Jane was surprised. "Can you tell me what it is and when it will happen?"

"No, we cannot," the one called Curly stubbornly responded. They were not supposed to interfere so were overstepping their galactic boundaries, as it was, by even warning Jane.

Jane had no idea what was going on; truth be told,

and she was not in the mood for their silliness. She just knew she was going crazy, was it the aliens, the weed, the bump on the head, her feelings towards Alice, or all the above. Everything was happening at once it seemed, like she was in a parallel universe. She wondered, was she the only one who could see the aliens? Were they a figment of her imagination?

"We'll be around when you need us Jane," she heard them say and then they were gone. She tried not to think of them as she went on about her duties of the day, even Alice eventually slipped her mind as her day got busy.

Chapter Five

JANE WAS GLAD THERE WASN'T A FULL MOON; people were crazier and things were worse when the moon was full. It was a fairly calm quiet day at work and Jane was most grateful for that. Only one domestic dispute called in and another rollover accident on the outskirts of town on that bad curve where they usually happen. It seemed people just could not get themselves to slow down and obey the forty-five mile per hour speed limit posted there. Before she knew it, it was five and time to leave work and head home. Jane was tired as she drove home. It was warm out so she dropped the top of her old convertible and enjoyed the warm breeze on her face and the wind whipping through her long hair which was determined not to stay tied back. She wanted to drive past the lane to her house and drive on through the open country side; but, she had to get home to feed her animals and water her garden. If only it would have rained as it was predicted she thought, then that would be one less thing she would have to do. She usually tried to check on her animals twice a day, and if she could not, she would ask her neighbor, Joyce, if she could come over to check on them. Joyce had a small farm too and many times they traded produce and planned their gardens accordingly so they would not get too much of any one crop. They shared a farmer's market stand in town on Sundays where they sold their homegrown organic produce.

Joyce was a little older than Jane, and had retired from the Post Office five years prior. She had bought her small farm while she was still working and living in town. Joyce had always delivered mail there and told the owners that if they ever decided to sell the farm and move to town that she would trade places. When the prior owner's health began to fail they took Joyce up on the deal; it was almost an even trade. Joyce was happily retired living on her small farm, just as Jane hoped to be very soon.

Joyce lived on the farm with her boyfriend, Pete, an older gentleman who had also worked at the Post Office and retired the same time as Joyce. But Pete went back to work part time at a chemical plant nearby. He was getting bored he said. He spotted the ad posted in the city diner one day. The pay they offered was so good he couldn't pass it up. The job was lab assistant and he worked four hours each evening. Joyce's kids and grandkids lived in Jefferson, a city about fifty miles away. Pete was divorced with grown kids of his own.

Pete had gone through a bad divorce some years earlier and didn't want to get married. Not getting married was fine with Joyce who liked being single; it gave her the illusion of being her own boss and decision maker. Pete and Joyce both loved horses and they would spend the early mornings riding horseback through the pastures, wooded areas and fields. On the weekends they would ride their horses over to Jane's farm bringing an extra horse along for Jane to ride. After a long ride they would come back to Jane's to have breakfast on her patio or go to Joyce and Pete's to eat. They liked to push back their chairs and chat and sip coffee after they ate. Most mornings, Jane's personal life was not brought up, unless Jane herself brought it up. Frankly, because Joyce and Pete had been there through Jane and George's divorce. They had heard enough whining, from both Jane and George. Seemed they both took turns, dropping by Joyce and Pete's place to vent. It's been long enough now, and Pete thought a boyfriend would be good for Jane.

****

It was a beautiful Saturday morning and they had just finished up their early morning brisk ride. Pete felt energized and fortunate enough to have Joyce in his life so he thought maybe their neighbor Jeff who lived on the farm on the other side of them, would be of interest to Jane. He certainly was handsome enough, Pete thought.

44

So he took a chance in bringing it up, after they ate, and were finishing their coffee.

"So Jane, I have a friend I would like you to meet; that is, if you are interested in dating again?"

"Oh, I still may not be ready for dating. I'm not over my divorce yet I don't think," Jane said feeling a dreaded lump in her stomach, suddenly thinking of Alice and having to face the fact that she had strong feelings for her. She had just removed the plates she had served the scrambled eggs and bacon on and had come back to the table to sit down. She felt that she should at least be polite and so she asked more about Pete's friend.

"What's his name," she asked trying to be polite enough to ask, as a vision of Alice suddenly popped in her head, that made her smile.

"His name is Jeff Holder and he lives right over the hill from us on a small farm," Pete said. "He's some kind of chemical engineer, a nice fellow. He does carpentry work as a hobby. He's done work for us. His wife recently died of cancer."

"Oh too bad," Jane was sympathetic and the subject was changed from Jeff to talk about cancer.

"Seems so many people are getting cancer these days." Jane frowned, then added,"I've read even the number of little kids getting cancer is on the rise, some are born with cancer. So sad!"

"I think it's all those pesticides and herbicides and genetically modified foods we eat where seeds are altered to withstand toxic chemicals. Or chemicals get sprayed directly onto the plants early on and then again before harvesting. And it seems these days that high fructose corn syrup, is in everything from animal feeds to most people foods," Jane said sounding disappointed and even a little angry. "I'm so glad that I have my garden, aren't you Joyce?"

"Yes I am," Joyce responded then went on. "I know the condition of my soil. I know what I plant and how I grow it. I don't blame the farmers. Farmers in the past were pretty much on their own, and held back grain to use as seed. They did not have to use all the chemicals like they have to today. But that's the big farmer with hundreds of acres, I'm just a little garden farm. I can hold back seed to plant the next season and grow potatoes from the sprouts of last season's potato crop. But some things are changing, I'm afraid. The potatoes that are sold in the stores now have chemicals on them so they will not grow sprouts," Joyce shared.

"Helping my aunt Ally plant straw potatoes was one of my happiest experiences as a child," Jane shared.

"Makes me feel as if 'they' want us to get sick!" Jane was downright mad now and continued her rant.

"Sorry to say but that is what it looks like to me." As Jane continued her voice got a louder. "Notice how 'they' control illnesses with lifelong medicines, but no cures, in so many cases," she added. Jane couldn't believe her own ears, that she was truly saying this. Yes, she read about this stuff and had her own theories, but she never expressed them verbally before now. Where was this coming from she wondered? If she would have thought a little harder she would have realized, it was the aliens putting words in her mouth. The thought did cross her mind, but surely the aliens would not do that, or would they? No wonder Jane was beginning to get a little concerned about her mental state.

"Okay, now you are depressing me," Pete said getting up from his chair after taking a last sip of coffee from his now empty cup. "I've always trusted the government to protect us and I believe that they do. I believe that this genetically modified organism stuff you are talking about is harmless." He smiled as he sat his coffee cup down and looked at Joyce in a way that asked, "Ready?" Joyce got up from her chair and trailed behind.

Jane noticed that Pete looked at her rather sternly as she went on her rant about the chemical companies. She had forgotten that Pete worked part time for a chemical company and his stern look reminded her.

"Joyce are you about ready to ride back?" Pete asked Joyce as he turned to walk over to the wooden fence to where the horses were tied. The horse jerked his head in protest as if he were content to continue eating the sweet tall grass that grew around the fence post. He snorted in protest, as Pete pulled his head around, led him away from the fence and then mounted the horse.

Joyce and Jane traded looks, both rolling their eyes at Pete's sudden strange change in attitude. They hugged each other goodbye quickly and then Joyce pulled herself up onto her horse.

"Okay Pete I guess we better get going, if we want to head over to Jefferson to visit the grandkids this afternoon."

"Are you staying over in Jefferson?" Jane asked.

"Want me to check on your animals and water your garden for you?" Jane offered.

"If something comes up and we do decide to stay, we will call you, but we are planning on returning this evening." Joyce thanked Jane for offering.

They thanked Jane for a lovely breakfast as they nudge their horses onward.

"I had fun this morning," she said and meant it and added that she would meet Jeff, Pete's friend, one day. And then her heart sank, because she dreaded that she said it, and dreaded the thought of them thinking that she actually may be interested in meeting their friend Jeff, as a possible dating partner. She found herself thinking more of Alice, her lovely blonde hair, her sweet smile and blue eyes. She wanted to get to know her better and not this Jeff person. The old traces of conditioned, social standards of everyone assuming you are straight, annoyed Jane. She should have just come right out and told Joyce and Pete that she was a lesbian; now, and always was, even when she was married to George. Oh, the word was hard for her to say, even to herself. Well, when you think that you are the only lesbian in the county, you become paranoid. But Alice had full out flirted with her saying she loved a woman in uniform, so that gave her hope.

Jane watched as Joyce and Pete rode off leading the horse she had ridden. They seemed so happy. She wanted to be happy too. She felt confused. Was it the bump on the head she received that confused her or that blonde. Did she have a concussion that she should have attended to? She didn't mention anything about it to Joyce and Pete. She certainly did not mention the alien visit. Pete and Joyce would have thought her crazy for sure and she wanted their friendship. She appreciated her neighbors, since her divorce, most of the friends she and George had shared now excluded her from their plans, so she was grateful for Joyce and Pete's friendship.

Chapter Six

The next morning while in the coffee shop across from the office, Jane noticed that there were a couple of Alice's flyers left on the bulletin board next to the door. She picked one up and looked it over.

"I just had my hair styled by Alice yesterday," the girl behind the counter at the register said. "What do you think?" she asked as he patted the back of her hair showing off her new hairdo.

"I really like it," Jane said smiling after looking over the clerk's hairstyle.

"I think maybe I need a new hairdo myself," she said grinning as she folded the flyer and stuck it in her pocket.

"Well, I like Alice. She's good at what she does and prices are reasonable. If you take that flyer with you to her salon you will only have to pay half price for any service."

Jane decided to go over to Alice's salon after she

got off work to make an appointment. The day passed slowly! She couldn't wait for five o'clock to roll around and it seemed like the end of her shift would never get there. Finally, when her shift was over, she quickly changed out of her uniform, and went up the street to Alice's salon. She felt shy and gingerly stuck her head inside Alice's salon door. She saw Alice putting a price poster up in the front window of her shop.

"Hello there, come on in," Alice immediately recognized Jane as the sheriff deputy who pulled her over and who she saw in the coffee shop. She thought Jane looked very attractive too even wearing street clothes. She looked pretty and Alice was happy to see her.

"Are you still open or were you about to close for the day?" asked Jane as Alice smiled and motioned for her to come in.

"I haven't illegally parked or anything have I?" Alice could not resist kidding Jane even though it was obvious she was not on duty. Jane was wearing nice white Capri style slacks and a black tank top and with sandals that showed off her pretty painted toenails. The sight of Jane moved Alice and her heart skipped a beat. Of course, being in the business her eyes scanned Jane's fingernails and toenails. She examined Jane's toe polish ever so nonchalantly and marveled at the neat job and pretty toes. Her look did not escape Jane's eyes and Jane was glad that she took the extra time to do a nice job. Alice always had her nails done up nicely; after all, you have to wear it, to sell it. Lots of ladies came into the shop and admired her polished nails, then wanted a manicure.

"What can I do for you today?" Alice asked, motioning for Jane to come sit in her dressing table chair.

"Oh, I think I need a trim. It's all grown out and just hangs without any style," Jane said looking at herself in the salon station mirror, holding out a long strand of hair to show Alice. Alice handed Jane a hand mirror as she turned the chair around so they both could look at the back of her hair.

"Looks like it needs to be layered. Well, okay, just sit back and relax and I'll see what can be done to make an already lovely lady, lovelier," Alice said with a smile. Jane tried to do what she was told to do, relax, but that was tough to do with Alice standing so close to her holding Jane's hair in both of her hands, running her fingers through it, to get the feel of the thickness, so she said. Alice wanted to see a reaction and she did, at that point Jane did not care at all what Alice did with her hair. She felt that she was in good hands and loved Alice's soft helpful demeanor not to mention her sensual touch. Finally, action was decided upon.

"Okay, I'll trim and shape it up," Alice suggested and after Jane agreed she thought maybe that more was needed, so she made another suggestion to go with the trim and style.

"How about some highlights while we are at it?" all the while massaging Jane's head as she spoke.

Jane just couldn't resist. Alice could have suggested shaving her head at that point and Jane would have agreed to it.

"Sure, why not," agreed a most relaxed Jane, "my

head is totally in your hands." Jane was looking in the salon station mirror and speaking to Alice's lovely reflection. Who could resist, she thought to herself.

"Great!" Alice was happy that Jane agreed to adding highlights. She loved when clients gave her free rein to try her creative suggestions. Her imagination went wild as she prepared to work: She got her supplies ready, wrapped a cape around Jane's shoulder, and mixed up the bleach in a bowl. They chatted about what Alice was about to do. Jane was a little uncomfortable when Alice pushed and tugged the tight fitting plastic cap with the tiny holes all over it on her head, but said nothing. Jane's eyes grew large with the look of surprise as Alice picked up what looked like a small crochet needle, and began to pull strands of her hair through the holes in the cap. It felt weird, but it didn't hurt. Jane watched Alice in the mirror as she worked and was mesmerized by her beauty. She felt high in her presence or was that the effects of inhaling the powerful fumes from the bleach mixture. Jane didn't care, she still trusted Alice, who could have colored her hair a bright chartreuse color and she would not have cared. She enjoyed watching Alice's reflection in the mirror magically performing her artistic talents. She smiled and every few moments Alice looked up and turned towards the mirror looking into Jane's eyes. Jane knew she was in love with Alice. She was smitten by Alice's wit, beauty, charm not to mention her hair styling talents.

Jane did not realize what was missing from her life until she met Alice. There was just something special about her, her grace, her beauty, and the way her hands felt on the back of her head and neck as she shampooed and dried the new hairdo. She loved her newly trimmed shoulder length highlighted hair. The highlights made her hair look three shades lighter. The change made her look ten years younger. When she came in had her dull graying brown hair. She blamed her ex-husband George for most of the gray hair, but he was out of her life now. It was time to turn a new and exciting page. Hopefully a new love relationship with Alice. Well, a girl can dream can't she?

"Oh, I love it!" Jane was excited about her new hairdo and smiled when Alice handed her the mirror and turned her chair around so she could see how nice the back flowed and bounced when she swayed her mop of heavy hair. Jane was sorry to see the two hours of hair care session end, during that time Jane had learned a lot about Alice. She had told Jane that she was all alone and new in town. She was lucky enough to be able to lease the apartment above the salon along with the salon. Since she settled in Hank she had spent every waking minute moving into her apartment and getting her salon set up. Jane loved listening to Alice and found that she did not want to say goodbye and have the visit end so she made a suggestion.

"So sounds like you have been very busy and not had a chance to look around town and see the sights, well what there is of them," Jane pointed out.

"No, I haven't had a chance to do much of anything," Alice said. She thought she knew where this conversation was headed and felt good about it. Alice was most curious about this tall attractive woman, with lovely hair, standing before her. Alice thought that she did a good job with Jane's hair and Jane liked it so that made her aching feet and sore back all worth it.

"You are my last appointment of the day and I'm hungry and thirsty, how about you?" Alice asked as she leaned against her work station. She was tired and resting on her elbows, then rising to get a better view as she pushed her blonde bangs away from her eyes. Backaches and sore feet were becoming the daily norm for Alice, the more popular she became, and the busier she got. Some days were more intense as she concentrated hard, trying to understand what a particularly difficult customer wanted. In her very short career of styling hair, she had found that most clients have an idea of what they wanted, but had difficulty trying to explain what they wanted. Jane was easy to please and for that she was most grateful. She especially liked Jane because Jane just let her do with her hair what she wanted, scoring multiple points. She thought Jane was hot, especially in her uniform but it was hard to beat the cute low cut neckline top and slimming capris and sandals Jane had on.

"Hey want a quick manicure and pedicure before we leave?" Alice offered. "It won't take long, fifteen minutes, top," Alice could see that Jane took care of her nails.

"Sure, if you feel up to it," Jane sat down at the manicure station while Alice gathered her manicure and pedicure supplies. Alice wanted Jane to look especially nice, because she had a crush on her. Besides Jane was walking advertisement for her salon, and every little bit helped to bring in more clients.

Alice at lease got to sit and be off of her feet while manicuring Jane's nails, and she was glad of that. She had graduated from cosmetology school about two years before and worked in several salons. But this was her first adventure in a new town and a shop of her own. She was so excited at the creative possibilities of having her own business and doing what she loved. When she wasn't styling hair, she was walking around the country side and through the streets of town taking pictures of scenery, historical covered bridges and buildings. She enjoyed walking in the rolling pastures and creeks or painting with acrylic on canvas the rich scenes that had captured her artistic eye. She wanted to see more and she wanted to get to know Jane better. She felt a special fondness for Jane, there was just something about her and they connected so well. Jane was instantly smitten with Alice as well and wanted to get to know her better too, hoping that Alice would find her just as interesting.

"Well, you look like you could use a treat. How about dinner at a great winery just up the road, right outside of town?" Jane was more than happy to get to know Alice better and Alice knowing that Jane was a county sheriff knew that she would learn a lot about the history of the area.

Jane drove Alice to the Vineyard Inn. A lovely restaurant settled in the grassy rolling hills outside of

Hank in southern Missouri. They followed the hostess to the patio where she led them to a small table for two. They were pleased that the hostess had led them near a cozy corner at the edge where they had privacy. The hostess sensed a look about Jane and Alice, as if there was something special between them so she showed Alice and Jane to their table. Jane and Alice thanked the hostess as sat down. They smiled as they took in the surrounding beauty, the various types of trees and plants that aligned the cobblestone patio, surrounded by ivy, thick and lush.

"I love your hair," the hostess complimented Jane, "it looks great!"

"Why thank you," Jane smiled turning towards Alice and nodding, "my stylist."

Alice smiled and reached into her handbag came out with a calling card she proudly handed the hostess. The hostess glanced at the card and slipped it into her skirt pocket glancing once again at Jane's hair.

"Hmm, I'll call for an appointment," she smiled as she handed Jane and Alice the wine list.

"Smart, business lady," smiled Jane and added, "I like that."

"It pays to advertise," smiled Alice. "Now, if I could only color and cut my own hair."

"You'll have to teach me," offered Jane.

"Deal," smiled Alice.

And they both giggled at the possibility of Jane learning to fix hair as they shared the single wine menu looking over the long list of possibilities.

They loved the scenic view from their table, looking out at the rolling vineyard hills and meadows. The setting sun created a rosy twilight glow on the valley. The evening air was warm with a just hint of an occasional cool breeze as the sun sank slowly in the west.

After some discussion and sampling of different wines they went with the waitress' suggestion, a popular fruity chardonnay. A string quartet began to play nearby just as the sun set orange and red in a mix of dark and light gray clouds. Alice "oohed" and "awed" and reached for her smart phone camera to capture the special moment of the evening glow, which cast a pinkness to their faces. The waitress noticed the opportunity and snapped pictures of Alice and Jane as they smiled leaning ever so comfortably close together. They followed the pose by clinks of glasses and sips of wine.

"Hmm, I think we chose well!" Alice said after taking another sip of wine. "Better bring me a glass of water too," she suggested to the waitress "I can feel the first sip go straight to my head already." Alice had not had any alcohol of any kind for months as she was too busy finding a new place to live and starting a new business. She felt so fortunate now to have met a new friend in a new town and beginning a new life. She had finally had a moment where she wasn't sad and grieving the death of her husband; maybe she was ready to get on with life again.

Jane was happy with her new do and her new friend. She felt that life was looking up since her divorce with

George. Alice was delighted. She had been in town for several weeks and Jane was the first client who really took an interest in knowing her. To celebrate the evening, they ordered filet mignon steak that was cooked to perfection. It was a lovely relaxing evening. They were enjoying dinner and listening to the strumming Latin sounds of the string quartet. They lingered chatting and listening until the music ended late into the evening. They were comfortable in their small talk and cozy intermittent silence vowing to visit a lovely Italian restaurant that Alice had seen advertised in the local paper on their next outing. Alice was beginning to enjoy the small tourist town of Hank, Missouri, Jane had made it very special for her.

"How did you come to choose to live in this crazy little town of Hank?" Jane asked.

"Believe it or not, my car broke down near Hank while I was on my way to visit friends in Arkansas. I had planned to move there from Springfield, Illinois after Joe died. I had to stay over in Hank while waiting for the parts for my car to arrive at the mechanic's garage. I was attracted to Hank somehow, the old town historical buildings of main street, the crafts, the artists, the farmers' market with the home grown foods and richness reflecting an earlier happier time. It just felt right so I looked at some business real estate that was for sale and found the available location on main street was perfect for my salon with living quarters above the shop. You, I met you. I guess it was destiny," smiled Alice.

"Yes, I believe in destiny," Jane agreed.

Jane had told Alice about her being psychic and intuitive besides being an obvious sheriff deputy. She told Jane about her small organic farm and contribution to the Sunday morning farmers market. She left out the fact that she had met and was visited by aliens — she did not want to freak Alice out, after all. Telling her about her alien friends could wait until a later date. Besides if she began talking about her alien visit, she might have to tell Alice that she is a hybrid and why she was one. She didn't think that the topic was ideal for first date conversation.

****

They had a lovely evening. Neither said anything but they both were thinking that they hated to see the evening come to an end. The time had gotten away from them and it was very late, so Jane drove Alice back to her little apartment above the salon. They smiled and said their goodbyes. Alice leaned over and kissed Jane on the cheek, then slid out of the passenger side of the car. Jane watched as Alice unlocked her apartment door and turned back to wave. Jane's heart pounded in her chest, after Alice's sweet kiss. She watched and made sure that she saw the light come on in Alice's apartment. Alice stepped out onto her living room balcony and waved to Jane. Jane waved in return, smiling.

"Good night."

"Good night."

It was as if neither of them really wanted to end the evening. Jane was still smiling as she drove out of town. She thought about Alice as she maneuvered the winding curves on the county highway that led to her farm. Her farm was always a welcome sight to her. She felt grounded and one with nature there. It was the family farm passed down through generations. She had no siblings so the hundred acres of crop fields, woods and pasture land was all hers. She raised goats for milk and keeping the yard manicured. She had chickens, a delightful garden with vegetables and fruit trees. A freezer and cold storage cellar in her log cabin promised wonderful organic meals all year round. She hoped Alice would like it and feel at home at the farm too.

She had such a lovely evening and she knew Alice did too. They promised to get together to try the Italian restaurant that Alice suggested. Conversation came so easy and they both enjoyed the same things, both were grateful for the company. Jane for one was getting tired of eating alone at the city diner close to the sheriff's office or cooking alone at home. Oh she loved the farm and her animals but she longed for interesting conversation. She and Alice talked about the changes in their lives and the difficulties of starting over in their fifties. Alice's husband's death and Jane's divorce were uncharted drastic shifts in plans for both of them. They both had to agree that just when you think you know what your future will bring then something happens to the plan and you have to pick up the pieces and begin again.

Jane continued her drive home down the narrow, bumpy, in much need of repair, county road off from the highway that led to her lane. The full moon lighted her way. The moon was bright and the sky clear of clouds so she could easily see the country side even though it was night. She had the top down on her old convertible it was a pleasant evening in the Ozark valley. As Jane drove along in the night heading home to her farm she enjoyed the cool breeze and the rhythmic sounds of the tree frogs in the trees and bushes that lined the ditch on either side of the road. The sounds were so soothing that she just didn't turn her car radio down, she turned it off, in order to embrace nature in all its glory, or was she just in love, maybe smitten by the blonde hair and blued eyed beauty, Alice. Her thoughts were drifting from past, to dreaming of the future, when she was suddenly jerked into the present by a strange sight.

The roadway was very dark and Jane had to swerve suddenly to avoid hitting a huge pot hole. After narrowly missing it, she looked up and was startled by a distant bright light in the sky. The light was coming closer. She shaded her eyes from the brightness when the light hovered in the sky several hundred feet above her. There was dead silence now. Jane pulled the car over to the side of the road and turned off her lights. She sat very still. She knew it was them, the aliens, watching her. She was curious to learn more about them. She was surprised that she was not afraid. The craft had huge bright amber colored lights that glowed on the ground beneath it. The light surrounded her. And then the space craft landed and there was movement on the ground coming towards her. She could tell that the figures were short, slender, pale, had big heads, huge almond shaped eyes, and as they got closer, she saw no visible ears, two small holes for a nose and a very small slit for a mouth. Yep, it was Moe, Larry and Curly alright.

Jane could have called the unidentified foreign object sighting in to dispatch and several patrol cars would have been there in minutes. But why all the commotion, she thought? Besides, Maggie, the dispatcher, would have thought that she was joking and would not have believed her anyway. Even though Jane had already met these aliens, she could barely believe what she was seeing. She blinked her eyes, yeah they were still there. They were standing on the other side of the ditch near the shiny round space craft. Jane did not know why her knees were shaking and her chest felt tight. She'd been in sticky situations before many times through the years being a deputy sheriff. But, she had to admit, that she had never experienced anything like aliens in all her thirty years of patrolling Hank County. Jane moved to open the driver side door, but before she could place her hand on the door handle, she felt the slight pressure of a hand placed on her shoulder.

"Jesus!" she whispered then turned slightly to her left only to stare into huge almond shaped eyes of an alien. The little slit of a mouth actually curved in a slight smile and the big head bowed as the alien removed his hand.

"You stay seated, Jane," the alien said and there

were two more standing behind the one speaking. They were smiling slightly which may her feel a little more at ease. The night was silent. The tree frogs and other night creatures Jane had listened to on her drive home remained silent. The night was quiet as if everything living had been mesmerized by these strange alien visitors. Jane's car engine had silenced and turned off. It was as if the Earth stood still waiting to hear what the alien visitors had to say.

"We are not Jesus, Jane." The one in the middle, called Larry said, "Although you hold this, so called, Jesus to great highs. We are flattered you think so highly of us, we are not this Jesus you speak of, though. By the way, you don't know this but you all here on Earth are Jesus. Mankind has been brainwashed by religious leaders in cahoots with government leaders, and big corporate leaders who say you are sick, weak, and helpless. You need this and you need that. They say this so that they are powerful over humankind and make hefty profits through your weaknesses. You are all mightier than what you are told. But you are easily fooled. You are pawns for their huge profits."

Jane took to heart what the alien said about Jesus and what religious principles had taught us. But, she was distracted by the fact that they were back visiting her again, so soon.

"So why me?" Jane was in awe of the these obviously far more advanced beings. She was more curious than afraid. Her heart raced with anticipation as she ventured into areas of the unknown. She sat quietly and listened to what they had to say; she was cautious and measured every word. She wanted to learn all that she could learn from these strange beings.

"There are many things, Jane, that we need to share with you," said the smallest of the three.

"Okay, I am ready to listen," Jane said and was truly eager to learn from these alien beings. She wanted to know their names.

"Tell me your real names. Do you have names?" Jane nervously asked while looking around to see if there were could be more of them coming out of the corn field following after these three that were standing at her driver side car door.

"I know your real names can't be Moe, Larry and Curly," Jane added.

"Our names are very difficult for humans to speak, so we say that our names are Moe, Larry and Curly," the one in the middle said and pointed with the longest of three thin digits on gray long slender hand, first at himself then to the alien on his left and then to the alien on his right.

"Don't tell me, a sense of humor, I love it," Jane said in a shaky voice barely above a whisper. She was shaken but kidding with them and happy to see that they were friendly.

"We know many things," said Moe the alien who stood in the middle of the three. He nodded his big head ever so slightly then continued in a rather high pitched, mechanical sounding voice that sounded like it came from deep inside his body.

"We are the guardians of planet Earth. We are under universal rule not to interfere with humankind's activities even though it may mean the annihilation of humankind and planet Earth. But, we are only alien and sometimes we cannot resist or we feel it is necessary to help prevent your destruction, so here we are visiting you again, Jane."

Jane got the feeling that the three aliens standing next to her car tried to mimic human emotions.

"So what are you three up to on this evening?" Jane was careful not to call them Jesus.

"Just cruising so a few can see our spacecraft. We are everywhere, we are invisible, we are your ancestors passed, we are your originators, we are your guides. We only come forth in the visible when we feel human beings need to know that there is more than what appears to be. Your religions taught you that you must believe in something you cannot see, your god. Your leaders hide us from you and created your god in their own image and likeness, to use as they see fit," explained Larry.

"Human beings know correct behavior from wrong behavior, yet greed, racism, hatred and wars for profit prevail all over the world. Stop the wars, stop the killings, stop the poisoning of food, soil, water and air." The alien, called Moe, made a slight smile with his tiny mouth and then continued, "Human beings need to learn to love each other and to love and protect the Earth. We have come forth in the visible to give you this message," Moe said.

"But what can I do with this message?" Jane said, feeling helpless and discouraged.

"Sheriff, we know that you are psychic, intuitive and substitute assistant editor in chief of your town paper. We know that you are respected and trusted. You have the means and will find a way."

"But I am only one woman in a small town," Jane insisted.

"Change comes from grass roots and spreads upward and outwards," the alien called Moe said.

Jane was thinking that she drank too much wine and was hallucinating; but, when she felt the bump on the back of her head she knew that she was not. She remembered all too well when she met these three aliens the night the prisoner had escaped.

"We just wanted to say hi Jane," the little alien named Larry smiled. "By the way, you better get home now, the goats are out of the fence again."

"Dang," crabbed Jane, "I just fixed that fence." She turned the key to the ignition, started the car, waved and pulled away slowly so as not to stir up dust on the three aliens.

The three waved with their long slender hands as Jane thanked them and drove off. This is really rather cool, Jane thought and smiled to herself. Nothing like having friends in high places, she thought. She could not believe that she was not afraid of them. The aliens told her that she was a star person herself. At this point, she thought, anything could be possible. She liked knowing that she and the planet had protection from the greedy corrupt groups, who just wanted to use up people and the planet for their own selfish personal gain. Where would the greedy go if they did wreck Earth, back to Mars? She had heard of space stations positioned near Mars, for the greedy to get back there one day, to their home, which was once livable and inhabited. She wondered if that were true, and if so, thought that it was probably the greedy who used up Mars until it was no longer inhabitable, and now were on planet Earth to continue their terror. Her train of thought switched from aliens, and Martians to herding goats when she pulled into her yard.

Jane found the goats on the outside of the fence just as the aliens had told her she would. It wasn't hard to spot the two white goats in the silvery moonlight. They were happily eating grass. Jane looked around and could see even in the moon light that there wasn't a weed in sight. They had been busy she thought. She walked slowly up to one of them and petted his head as he busily ate, then slipped her hand under his collar and attached the long dog lease to the ring. He bucked at her in protest then grabbed one last mouthful of the tall grass that he had been munching on. Jane gently tugged at the lease and managed to pull him away from the grass. She led him inside the gate and into the barn to join the two goats that didn't venture out, and then she went back out and got hold of the other goat and led him back into the barn. She made sure all of her animals were in for the night. She closed and double checked the latch to the barn door. With flashlight in hand, she quickly searched and discovered their escape route through an opening in the gate wiring. She temporarily patched it with wire and vowed to get up early in the morning to further secure it.

Jane walked back through the yard cautiously through dark shadows to the house. She felt a little creeped out because most areas of her yard were not illuminated by the single yard light. When she reached the house she went inside and thought about getting ready for bed but realized that she was not a bit tired. Maybe a mug of hot chocolate would relax her and make her sleepy. She prepared it from a package and hot water heated in the microwave and went to sit on the front porch that faced the corn field beyond her front yard that ran along the lane that led down to the county road. Once again, the night was filled with night sounds of tree frogs. She could hear owls in opposite directions conversing back and forth. The night was back to being noisy and she decided the space craft was gone—for now. As she sipped the hot chocolate, she sat very still just listening. She believed that she was still in shock; it's not every day aliens in a flying saucer come to visit you. She sat on front porch for a while contemplating the wonderful evening she had spent with Alice and the extra special treat of seeing the aliens again. She was not afraid of them and felt like part of them even though they looked so different.

She peered up at the night sky and spotted the flashing silver light shining off of a space craft as it streaked across the night sky. She watched the saucer tip slightly to one side, like a gentleman would tip the brim of his hat to a lady while saying goodnight. The sight warmed her heart. She took a last sip and finished up her hot chocolate before it got cold, then went inside to head up stairs to bed. She climbed the creaking pine steps up to the loft bedroom where she planned to sleep for the night. After meeting with the aliens, she wanted to be up high, and closer to the stars so she chose the loft over the master bedroom below her on the main floor. She wanted to lie in bed and stare up through the sky light into the starry night. She changed into her pajamas and crawled into bed. She laid there in hopes of seeing another flyby from her friends. From the loft, she could see everywhere in the house below her. She could see into the livingroom and part of the kitchen in the corner of the house. She felt safe and connected in the loft being twelve feet closer to the Pleiades star cluster. The sky light in the roof faced in the Northeast direction and she could see six of the seven sister stars that make up the Pleiades star system. Jane, being a hybrid, felt a strong connection to the brightest star, Alcyone, as the point of her origination. She laid warm and cozy under the quilted covers as she stared through the sky light window, through the splintered treetops, into the starry sky. She was looking for them, the aliens, her friends. She thanked the universe for her blessings, her little farm, her cabin, for Alice. She was excited by the thought of someday showing Alice her little farm. She hoped Alice liked the farm and the country and she hoped Alice was not afraid of meeting aliens.

Chapter Seven

It was Saturday morning and Jane slept in. When she awoke, she couldn't think which day of the week it was. Then she heard a brisk knock at her back door. Jumping out of bed and looking over the loft railing, she saw Joyce and Pete on the porch peeping through the window. She hustled to throw on her jeans, shirt and boots and was downstairs in a flash and unlocked and opened the back door.

"Oh, oh, think we woke you up, didn't we?" Pete smiled at Jane's uncombed hair and untucked shirt.

"Why don't you come in and fix some coffee for yourselves while I finish up," Jane suggested. She was happy to see warm friendly faces.

"I must have been really sleeping," she added feeling a little embarrassed while running her fingers through her hair trying to smooth the tangles.

"You take your time, we'll fix the coffee," Joyce said

as she moved in the kitchen and looked in the cupboard. She had been in Jane's kitchen many times and knew where the coffee, cups and everything she needed were located.

"I have donuts too!" Jane pointed to the kitchen counter where the box sat as she turned to go down the hall to the bathroom.

"Oh, these look great," Pete said as he reached for one of the glazed donuts in the box. He was hungry and glad to see that Jane had a least a half dozen big donuts, just the kind he liked too, the kind with a light glaze. He hated the heavily glazed type, He was watching his weight after all, "can't get too big to ride my horse," he often would say. Besides he wanted to not only watch his weight but stay healthy. So many of his golfing friends were overweight, causing them to get sick with diabetes and high blood pressure. He did not want to have to be on medications. He had read about the serious debilitating side effects of pharmaceutical drugs, even watching the commercials gave him a creepy feeling. He had already refused to take statins after his doctor suggested he take them for preventive purposes even though he did not have a high cholesterol problem. He and Joyce did not always agree on everything, but they bought agreed that they did not want to get in the vicious cycle of taking prescription drugs. Unbeknownst to Joyce, Pete already worked with dangerous chemicals at his job. Pete felt that he had enough exposure to toxicity at work to even consider the risks of adding more to his system. But, this morning, Pete's mind was

72

on horseback riding and enjoying a beautiful day. He was feeling particularly well and smiled and joked with Joyce while drinking coffee and munching on a donut while waiting for Jane to finish getting ready.

Joyce and Pete had just poured a second cup of coffee, as Jane came out of the bathroom, dressed and ready to take on the day. She looked fresh as the morning dew with light makeup applied and her lovely streaked hair tied back in a colorful silky scarf.

"Oh, I love the highlights," smiled Joyce. Now that Jane's hair was combed she could see them.

"Yes, new hairdresser in town," said Jane turning around, "I really like her," and she meant that in more ways than one. Jane was all smiles as she grabbed a donut and filled a cup with coffee.

"How about we'll just eat a little now, and after the ride through the woods, ride over to our place for ham and eggs when we are finished? The ride will take about three hours. We'll be hungry again by then I'm sure," suggested Pete as they finished their donuts and coffee. Pete was average height and slender, as was Joyce; they were in their fifties, but they looked and acted more like people in their thirties. Jane thought that they made a cute couple. She loved having them for neighbors. With the mention of later breakfast, she only ate one donut, thinking she really wanted to watch her weight; after all, she wanted to impress Alice. Alice had a great figure. Jane couldn't get Alice out of her mind and just stared into space as she leaned against the kitchen sink finishing the last bits of her donut.

"Earth to Jane?" Pete smiled and shared a sideways glance with Joyce.

"Oh, guess I'm still half asleep," Jane stammered and came back to reality. She didn't tell them that she was thinking about Alice, sweet Alice. She finished the last sips of her coffee, rinsed out the cup, grabbed her cowboy hat and they were out the door.

It was a lovely morning for horseback riding, she had looked forward to it all week. The air was crisp and cool, and the grass glistened with dew. She was excited about her evening with Alice the night before; even the alien visit could not over shadow her lovely evening with Alice. Well it could, she had to be realistic, but only by a narrow margin. She was sure that Joyce and Pete could sense her happiness but she did not elaborate, she wasn't quite ready to share those treasured moments with them, just yet. With thoughts of the Aliens and Alice, Jane guided her horse through the meadows. Joyce and Pete trailed close behind. They were enjoying the quiet of the morning and the warm sun on their faces. They listened to the birds calling one another as they rode through the hills and meadows of pastureland.

They had been riding for quite a while when Pete spoke up and broke the silence.

"You haven't met our neighbor Jeff yet have you?" Pete asked. Pete had spoken of Jeff several times before on their weekend morning horseback rides. Pete thought Jeff was a very interesting guy, and Joyce thought he was handsome. He lived on the other side of their property on a small farm. They felt they all had a lot in common, Jeff even had horses.

"No, I have not met him yet, why didn't you bring him along on the ride?" Jane asked.

"I did ask him. He said that he had an early appointment of some sort and maybe would join us another time," answered Joyce. "We have mentioned it to him several times before,.

They slowed then to walk their horses across a rocky stream. After they reached the other side, Joyce continued, "He's a nice guy, he's planning on joining us for breakfast if he gets back in time. Hope that is alright with you?" Joyce's eyes met Jane's.

"Oh, that's fine," Jane said lightly. "You two have spoken of him so often that I feel like I know him already."

She only hoped that they would not think she was happy because of the prospect of meeting Jeff. It was Alice that she was all smiles about.

"So what did you do last evening, anything special?" Joyce asked as they guided their horses through the pasture leading them on the etched out cow paths that meandered through the grassy pastures hills and along the creek.

"Oh, I went out to dinner with Alice, after she finished with my hair. She is new in town and I showed her around a bit. We went to the winery just outside of town," answered Jane. "We had a very nice time. She's very nice."

"And talented," Joyce added and Pete smiled in

agreement. Jane thought she caught them looking at each other then. Did they sense her special feelings she had for Alice? She wondered but not enough to really care what Joyce and Pete thought.

"You know a new hairdo can change you into a totally different person," she smiled and Joyce and Pete laughed and looked at each other with raised eyebrows sensing there was more going on than just a new hairdo.

Jane wanted to shout from the roof tops about her feelings for Alice but she had to contain her emotions. She was afraid Joyce and Pete might not understand. Heck, she never even smoked weed around them and the topic never came up in conversation. She had to be careful as she was a sheriff's deputy after all. As they rode the horses through the pastures and meadows of thick rich grass and wild sunflowers, Jane's mind was on Alice. She attempted idle conversation with Joyce and Pete but preferred to just listen and chime in every once in a while with a "ah" or "hmm" just to appear interested but her mind was on Alice.

Jane forced herself back into the present, as they rode over to Joyce and Pete's yard and she saw that they had a visitor. Leaning against Pete's pickup truck was a tall, thin cowboy. His hat was pulled down low over his eyes. He stood with arms folded, long legs crossed at the ankles. He stared at the pretty woman on horseback, with long pretty hair tied back under a cowboy hat. Blue denim shirt and long legged jeans straddling a golden brown mare was a sight to see. It was quite obvious that the cowboy was moved at the sight of the lovely lady and how she easily handled the horse she rode. He stood tall then and took a step closer so he could get a better look at the lovely lady he was about to meet.

"Hello," Jeff said and Jane couldn't help but stare at his tan rugged looks and pearly white teeth that glistened when he smiled; but, bells and whistles were going off in Jane's head. There was something a little off she thought, something she saw in his eyes. He spoke kind words, even flirted a bit, she thought, but his eyes told another story, one of secrecy and mystery. Jane's intuitive senses had been sparked for only a few seconds and she soon forgot about it. She wanted to be friendly, but conversation began difficult after idle chitchat about horseback riding and the weather. An obvious low in the conversation occurred which Pete tried to fill.

"You should have come earlier and joined us for a ride this morning," Pete said smiling. Jeff smiled back in return, while lifting the brim of his cowboy hat as if to get a better view of the folks in front of him, but mainly to get a better look at Jane.

Jane felt Jeff's eyes settle on her and linger. She felt uncomfortable. Suddenly she lost her appetite. But she was going to be stuck there unless she got an emergency call from the dispatcher regarding some police problem, and that was so unlikely to happen in this quiet county.

"Jeff, this is Jane," Joyce said introducing them.

Both Jeff and Jane appeared slightly embarrassed because it was obvious to them that it was indeed a fixup breakfast. They smiled at each other and each knew that they were going to go along with the charade.

"Hi, Jeff," Jane said as he smiled and lightly took hold of her hand then took the reins from her and led her horse to the stables. From there Pete took over and loosened the saddle straps. Jane thought she saw Jeff wink at Pete as if he liked what he saw in her. Jane's heart sank. She had been married to George and had crushes on women throughout their marriage. She was not about to repeat that same scenario. She could tell he liked her. This was going to be a problem, she thought.

In the kitchen as Jane helped Joyce prepare breakfast she silently argued within herself. Why was she so worried about what people thought and about pleasing other people anyway? Maybe it is time she pleased herself.

Breakfast was delicious and Jeff vowed to ride with them the next weekend and then he mounted his horse to ride back to his farm. Jeff wasn't much of a horseman until Joyce and Pete moved onto their farm with their horses. They had six horses total and soon Jeff and his wife began riding with them and adopted two of their horses.

"So what do you think of Jeff?" Joyce asked Jane later on after Jeff left.

"Well, he's handsome," Jane said as she shared her feelings and observation. But then thought that she should be truthful and tell Joyce and Pete about her feelings about Alice. After all Joyce and Pete seemed like open minded, kind people. They weren't religious, racist or bigoted in any way that Jane could tell and she had known them for ten years. They had been very understanding and kind through Jane's divorce and she appreciated that.

Many a night they were patient enough to listen to Jane cry over emotionally abusive George. She and George had met Joyce and Pete one day as they rode their horses passed her farm and stopped to welcome them to the neighborhood after they moved in. Pete and Joyce hated to see them split up and never quite understood though what broke up Jane and George's marriage.

Jane had tried to explain to Pete and Joyce, then, that George had changed after he went to work for the new chemical company in the county. He had changed; he got ugly. They argued all the time and then he got home later and later until he it got to the point where he was never home. Jane thought that he was lying when he said he was forced to work late. She thought that George was having an affair. Of course, she thought that out of a guilty conscious because she had had an affair. Jane had had a crush on a fellow woman officer. They had a brief affair. They were careful, they thought. But then one day, the woman, her name was Peggy, no longer showed up at work, and Jane found out that Peggy was moved to a different shift. Jane rarely saw her and when she did, it was only at shift change. Peggy barely looked at her. Jane tried to talk to her to no avail. And then one day she was gone and the captain said that Peggy and her husband had moved to another town. Jane was left lonely and heartbroken. George was angry when he found out and said he wanted a divorce.

Jane brought herself back to the present and decided not to say anything more about Alice yet. She thanked them for breakfast and they parted ways for the day.

****

The next morning Joyce and Pete rode their horses to Jane's house along with a horse for Jane to ride. It was a nice morning and they thought they would swing by, bringing a horse with them for Jane in case she wanted to ride with them.

"Where's Jeff this morning?" Jane asked and looked around on the porch as she opened the door for them.

"He said he was expected at work, that something had come up, something unexpected," Pete reported.

"Oh, too bad," Jane said as she pulled herself up onto the mare she usually rode. She patted the side of her neck. The mare was ready to go, as were the other two horses.

"So what did you think about Jeff?"

"Straight out of the movies, that one," smiled Jane.

"We thought you might think that he was good looking," offered Pete.

"Well, I must say he is, but then I must say, that I find women attractive, too," Jane spilled out, and then silence fell. Why had she said that? You could have cut the silence with a knife. She hoped Pete would not think she meant Joyce.

"Are you hitting on my wife?" Pete accused Jane, although he was smiling big and showing sparkling white teeth against a deep bronze tan. When Jane responded with a blank look he added, "Keep in mind, I saw her first," then laughed out loud as Joyce turned red.

"Hey, no fighting over me!" Joyce laughed.

"Darn, and as attractive as Joyce is, I do realize that she is already taken."

Jane smiled, happy they were making this easy for her, "Really, I have another woman in mind." Jane was happy to be honest about her feelings and to talk about Alice.

"Now I'm jealous!" exclaimed Joyce, sounding more than a little disappointed; she wasn't smiling.

"Tell us more," Pete urged Jane, suddenly very curious.

"Her name is Alice. She is the new hair stylist in town." Jane smiled and blushed also as if she was surprise at her attraction for Alice.

"There is just something about her," Jane had to confess.

"Oh, I must check her out. I think I need a haircut," smiled Pete as he guided his horse around a stump protruding boldly out on the trail in the front of him.

"Well, I'm going with you then," Joyce wasn't going to allow Pete to go alone.

"Hey, I saw her first!" Jane smiled then laughed repeating the same phrase Pete had used earlier. She was glad they appeared to be at ease but then there was a long moment of silence with everyone seeming to be into their own thoughts. Finally, Joyce was the first to break the silence.

"Well, you must keep us updated," suggested Joyce as they neared Jane's yard.

They vowed to ride again the next weekend. Jane said that she would plan on it; she was looking forward to it already. But now she had to hustle to do a few things around the farm before getting ready to go to work the evening shift. She had just enough time to feed the animals and pick a few things from her garden for her evening salad at lunch break. As she headed up to her house, she watched Joyce and Pete ride off in the distance leading the horse that she had ridden. She wondered what they were talking about; probably her, she thought. She was glad that she opened up to them and glad that they were opened minded. She thought that they sounded genuine too.

Chapter Eight

Jane thought that everything was going smoothly and she was happy with her life: She had great neighbors. She had a wonderful relationship with Alice. Her work was usually calm and quiet, and she was nearing retirement. She had forgotten about her ex-husband, George, and his threats at the time of their divorce two years ago, now the threats seemed to have been fruitless and idle sarcasm. Time heals all or so she thought.

Later, she guessed those thoughts were a premonition of what was to come, for the very next evening she found a letter from George in her mailbox. As soon as she saw the all too recognizable handwriting her heart froze with fear. There was no mistaking that the letter was from George. She knew all too well the way he printed a's to look like crooked z's. The letter had no return address and no stamp or postmark. This meant that he had hand delivered it himself. The idea that

George was roaming around her property had her literally shaking in her boots. Jane became frightened and wondered what was going on, she carefully opened the envelope as she slowly walked back to the house from the mailbox, almost stumbling several times on the uneven rocky lane trying to read and walk at the same time.

Something fell out the envelope face down onto the ground. It looked like the back of a photo. When she picked it up and turned it over, she felt suddenly lightheaded and almost fainted and the photo slipped from her hands. She waited a moment and then bent over to pick up the photo again. Feeling slightly better, she proceeded to examine the horrid picture. He hand was shaking. It took her a minute to realize that the photo was a picture of George. He looked awful. He was practically bald with only small patches of thin graying hair. His cheeks were hollow. He looked close to death, Jane thought. She hurried to read the letter that was enclosed.

"Jane, I had to send you this picture of me so you would know what has happened to me. After we divorced and I moved away, I took a job in the lab at a seed and chemical company. I have discovered many things there that I am afraid to talk about. Although, what does it matter now? My exposure to the chemicals, that are used there, have made me dreadfully sick with cancer. When I die I want you to have a private autopsy performed and expose the truth to the public. I have kept hidden many of the documents that will prove what I say is the truth. I am in hiding right now. Others who had gotten sick, and realized what made them sick, are dead. The media has been paid off, as well as local officials. The company's toxic sweetener products are in most all the foods that are sold and eaten. The sweetener is supplied to all food manufacturers at such a low price that the company is guaranteed of its usage. This product is in everything from bread to baby food. When I was first hired we were provided three meals a day and all expenses paid. We were living on the premises. I should have realized that I was a hired guinea pig and that they were testing their food products on a small group of us. They did not have to wait very long; it seems that within fifteen months I was sick. The other people in the group were gone because after fifteen months they split us up. They moved me to another position at another location. So I have no idea how the other people are doing. I suspect that I am being watched, so I had a trusted friend have someone to deliver this envelope to you. I have no one else to turn to. For your safety you will not know my location; more details to follow. In the meantime, trust no human. I apologize."

That was it. George kept the note very brief and without means of identification of himself or Jane. The fact that he wrote, "trust no human" struck a chord with Jane. Who knew about what was going on and were keeping it secret? Trust no human. Then Jane thought of the aliens that had contacted her and knew that she was a substitute coeditor of the local paper. But how could a substitute coeditor of a local paper help?

Jane's intuition told her that her whole world changed and that nothing would be the same ever again. "Well, there went that peace of mind I thought I finally had," she said to herself.

****

Jane stopped at the local newspaper office to do a little editing on the weekly paper while on her way to work. There were notices of deaths and pending funerals, and pending estate sales. She looked through the ads. One ad, in particular caught her eye, it was lumped in with ads for garden supplies, church festivals, and softball scores. It was an ad for hiring lab technicians with no experience required, with on the job training, at a plant called MARTA located near the next county. The ad listed an address and a phone number. Jane was intrigued of course. Was this the place? Was she about to become a reporter, a detective, a spy and a lab technician, or none of the above, and run for the hills? She had to put it to the back of her mind and went on with her work.

Jane's patrol rounds were pretty routine that evening, just one spousal abuse call. The wife was a first time caller, the husband was drunk and Jane stayed a bit while she advised them as they talked things over. The husband promising to stop drinking. Jane thought that she would probably get another call in the future from the woman, but hoped she was wrong. Her shift ended at ten and she headed home thinking about men and husbands, her ex-husband and risky jobs. She quickly pushed the negative aside and concentrated her thoughts on Alice. It was a beautiful star filled night as she dropped the top to her convertible. She wished Alice was with her, coming home with her, how sweet that would be. She missed Alice, and was happy that she had dinner plans with her for the next evening.

Jane's thoughts were on Alice as she drove home after work. She turned off the main highway and heading down the county road leading to her farm. The night was well lit by the full moon, and she could easily see the houses and fields along the side of the road as she drove past them. She was within two miles of her farm when she spotted a silvery sleek disc-shaped craft carefully parked in a field on the right side of the road. Little twinkle lights that aligned the craft were flashing enough to highlight the small alien beings walking towards the road. She felt them, their thoughts, summoning her to bring her car to a stop. While pulling over to the side of the road, she immediately thought of George's note and what the aliens had predicted she would be doing and it was beginning to make sense now. She turned her engine off and waited for them to approach her car.

"I must be one of these aliens," Jane said out loud to herself, "because, why am I not afraid of them?" Jane felt perfectly comfortable around Moe, Larry and Curly as they jokingly called themselves. She had asked, but they told her their real names would be too difficult for her to pronounce. Really, with names like that, who could take them seriously she wondered but yet she wanted to, and so believed them. She sensed their thoughts and felt that she and they were here to help save the Earth and its inhabitants from Earthly evil doers.

She immediately recognized Moe as he approached her car with Larry and Curly trailing closely behind. Here they came comically heading to her car with their prancing little steps, arms proudly swinging, big heads bobbing a bit with each step and huge almond shape eyes looking over Jane as if this was the first time they had seen her.

"What's up boys?" Jane smiled as the three walked through the shallow ditch and rounded her car to the driver's side. Moe was the first to speak.

"We know you got that note from George," Moe said and he saw that what he said startled Jane.

"Not to worry Jane, we know all things. We are keeping an eye on you. Even when you do not see us, we see you," contributed Larry.

"Well what can you do to help?" Jane wanted to know.

"We are pledged via universal galactic rules not to interfere. We only supposed to watch and advise," explained Curly.

"Well I could use some advice," pleaded Jane, "is there anyone of you who can help me? Do you know what I should do?"

"No, sorry," said Larry and Curly snickered from behind him. They had funny ways, these aliens.

Jane felt helpless as she watched the Aliens get back

into their craft. She watched as the craft, rose, hesitated slightly, tipped a goodbye then in a flash, vanished into the night.

"Hey no fair not helping!" Jane called after them. Somehow she knew that she would be seeing them again and soon. In her mind she knew that if she really truly needed their help they would help her. She knew they were just playing with her. Jane was tired and glad to be home. She pulled the car into the barn next to her old pickup. Did a quick walk around to check on the animals then went into the house where she went straight to bed. She felt a little sad. She missed Alice. She needed cheering up and looked forward to the plans she had made with Alice for the next evening. She was so excited it took her a while to fall asleep but when she did she dreamed sweet dream of Alice.

****

Jane came through the beauty salon door just as Alice was about to turn the "open" sign around to the "closed for the day" side.

"Hey there you are; come on in," Alice was happy to see Jane and took her by the arm and led her inside.

"You look very nice," Alice said as she kissed Jane on the cheek.

"Oh this old thing," Jane laughed at her own using of an old cliché'. She had slipped out of her deputy uniform into a gray skirt, red blouse and sandals before she left the office. She untied and brushed out her long hair.

"I think I may need a trim soon," Jane said observing herself in the salon station mirror, "but not tonight. Tonight we wine and dine."

"Sounds good to me," smiled Alice. "I've been standing on my feet styling hair all day, and bending over this shampoo bowl is a back killer. I'm not complaining, mind you, but I am ready to wine and dine." Alice smiled as she led Jane out of the shop door, turning the lights off as she went out.

They had made plans to try to the Italian restaurant that Alice suggested. Jane had her convertible top down and the weather was perfect for it. The warm night breeze caressed their skin. They arrived at the restaurant in minutes and the hostess seated them at a table on the patio and handed them a drink list. It was good to relax after a busy day. They ordered a fine bottle of Malbec from Argentina. And the waiter had just brought it to them, and filled their glasses before setting the bottle back in the chilled holder. They leisurely looked over the menu before both deciding on the lasagna Bolognese dish one of Alice's clients had suggested.

"To us!" Alice held her glass up and Jane tapped the rim with hers repeating, "to us." Jane immediately wanted to lean over and kiss Alice. She was surprised at her sudden flow of desire. She needed a release from the stress of George's note, and she wondered if she was the only one around the county who saw Aliens and were visited by them regularly. No matter what was going on, tonight she was going to forget about everything else, except enjoying this lovely blue-eyed blonde sitting next to her.

"I'm so glad we are here together," Jane said and meant it with all her heart.

"So, how was your day?" Alice asked Jane.

"Long actually. Working the day shift is usually busier. But it seemed slow today," Jane said and admitted, "it seemed slow because I was waiting to be with you"

"Me too," smiled Alice "I thought five o'clock would never come."

Their food came then, and more wine was poured and sipped between the bites of salad and lasagna which both declared most delicious. After dinner they remained seated and shared another bottle of wine. The sun was just setting behind glowing clouds of purple and orange and yellows casting a pinkish glow on Alice's pretty smile.

"You look adorable in this light," Jane whispered. She couldn't help it, between the gorgeous sunset and pretty Alice it just came out.

"Why, Jane are you hitting on me?" Alice had just enough wine to flirt and mean it.

"Why yes, I suppose I am," smiled Jane becoming almost suddenly nervously surprised at her daringness. Then she thought, "hell I get mysterious notes from my dying ex, aliens come to visit me and I just came out as a lesbian—my life might as well be complete."

"I'm glad," smiled Alice, moving closer.

"Want to leave?" Jane asked her heart racing.

"Want to come to my apartment?" invited Alice. It was the closest place for them to drive to, Jane's farm being a few more miles away in the opposite direction. They paid their bill hurried to the car and held hands while Jane drove, their long hair blowing in the wind and both lost in thoughts of what was to come.

Alice kissed Jane as they climbed the steps and entered her living room.

Their kisses were deep and wanting. Alice led Jane to her bedroom where they stayed making love till the early morning light. Alice woke and realized that she had an early morning appointment and Jane had to get home to tend to her animals. Jane had the day to do what she needed not having to be back at work until three o'clock in the afternoon.

Jane felt as if she was floating on air, she was so in love with Alice. There was a beautiful sunrise that morning. She had the convertible top down enjoying the warm breeze through her long hair as she drove out of town. She turned off the main highway onto the county road leading to her farm. Jane thought as she drove through the pastures and corn fields how she loved living in the country on her farm. Up ahead she saw the train coming. Yes, she loved her farm out in the country, but she was not so fond of having to wait at the crossing for the approaching train. But today she was high on love and she didn't even mind because it just gave her more time to think about Alice. The train was slow but being pulled by only one locomotive engine meant there would be only about ninety tankers, boxcars, and coal cars coming around the bend and soon the train would be gone and she could get on home. The trains always slowed here before the sharp bend. George always said this would be a good place for hobos to jump on and off the box cars which always had the doors open. Jane thought of what George said when she saw the train is going very slow and box cars empty and doors left open apparently after the goods were delivered. Jane had no idea why she even thought of hobos, or of George, between her loving thoughts of Alice. She pushed them out of her mind because she only wanted to have happy, loving thoughts of Alice. They vowed to see each other over the weekend. Jane switched her future work schedule to day time hours so she could spend more evenings with Alice. The train had finally passed, and she drove across the tracks and continued home. She couldn't stop her heart from pounding in her chest. She had never felt this way before about anyone, certainly not George she thought. Her thoughts turned then to George and she worried about him. Her feelings of worry for George surprised her. She wondered what she could possibly do to help him. There was not much she could do until he sent her more information she guessed. Little did she know that more information was on its way.

Jane was enjoying the early morning cool air. She slowed to pull up to her mailbox to get the mail from the day before. When she opened the mailbox door she found a gold envelop inside she hesitantly pulled it out of the box. It was addressed to her without a return address or postage stamp which meant this envelope too was hand delivered. The idea that someone had been this close to her personal space gave her the creeps. She was afraid to walk into the house and the out buildings, yet she knew she had to go tend to her goats, chickens and garden. Jane searched through the out buildings and the house for anything out of the ordinary, misplaced or disturbed. When she was satisfied that nothing was touched and that there had been no intruder, she settled down on the couch with a glass of tea and the large yellow envelope addressed to her with the same silly printed letters, the "a" looking like a "z".

She carefully tore open the edge of the envelope and peered inside. There were numerous sheets of handwritten and typed papers. What she saw appeared to be a log of testing procedures on certain chemicals with plants and animals and all results appeared to be the same: highly toxic. Evidently the company knew that the chemicals being used in foods products was toxic but exposed humans and animals to them in products sold all over the world. Jane could not believe what she was seeing. She had no clue as to how to go about protecting this information or exposing this information. She had no idea what was expected of her. Was there even a correct party to give this too or were all forms of government agencies already aware of what was going on. After all, chlorine gas and Agent Orange were knowingly used on humans during war, what would make this any different, Jane thought. Well someone knows that I have this information because they gave it to me, why didn't they just go forward with it and leave me out of this? Jane was in no mood to be a hero. She felt helpless mostly, who was she to go after the big guys with big guns anyway? And doesn't the public really know already but just fail to face the facts. She felt outnumbered and unqualified to mess with this. She had no idea who she could trust. Could she even trust her captain, Mike, or her neighbors Joyce and Pete or Jeff? She thought maybe her job was just to hide this information for George and that was all that she could do for him.

Chapter Nine

THE WORK WEEK CAME AND WENT QUICKLY and suddenly it was Saturday morning. Joyce, Pete and Jeff rode over for their usual horseback ride and Jane happily joined them. After the ride she asked Pete and Jeff to unload some chicken feed while they were at her farm.

"Why are you buying chicken feed?" asked Jeff.

"Well, I bought too many chickens and they ate all the grass, I thought my grassy pen would be big enough, but without enough rain, the grass growth cannot keep up." Jane's plan was to raise chickens to butcher, to sell, along with eggs at the local farmers' market.

"I was thinking about getting some chickens myself," Jeff said walking down the backdoor porch steps, "but now I'll just buy them from you, eggs too."

"Yes, plan on it!" Jane was happy to hear she already had a standing customer.

As Jeff walked out Jane noticed that Joyce seemed

eager to talk girl talk with her. While Pete and Jeff were unloading the truck for Jane, she and Joyce had a chance to catch up on some girl talk. Jane was surprised to learn, that Pete and Joyce really did not know much about Jeff.

"He doesn't talk much about himself only that his wife had died from cancer and so did his little girl." Joyce said, but then she quickly changed the subject. She wasn't interested in talking about Jeff; she wanted to hear more about Jane and Alice's relationship.

"Have you seen Alice lately?" asked Joyce, intrigued about Jane having a relationship with a woman. She thought Jane appeared sleepy, but very happy, on their ride that morning.

"Why, as a matter of fact I have. We had dinner at that new Italian restaurant last evening," Jane said with a big smile as Joyce encouraged her to share more information.

"And then?" Joyce was not interested in hearing anything about the new restaurant in town rather she wanted to know how Alice was.

"Oh, Alice invited me to her apartment afterwards," smiled Jane, actually eager to share the information.

"Oh, no wonder you were smiling this morning!" Joyce was more than slightly jealous. She really wanted to ask Jane more, but didn't know if Jane was ready to talk about such intimate details with her, not just yet anyway. Joyce did not want to admit it to herself, certainly not to Jane, but she was attracted to Jane. Maybe she and Pete had just been married too long and she needed a spark.

Alice was coming for dinner that evening and Jane felt that she had a lot of work to do to make her place look especially presentable to Alice. Alice's apartment was so nice and tidy. She was an artist after all, Jane thought, wishing she had designer talents. Alice had her place decorated mostly in Earth tones with red, orange and yellow accent pieces. Jane looked around at her place and thought it looked old and outdated. She knew she was feeling this way, because Alice was coming over. Still, she really wanted to impress Alice so she had spent every evening for the past week cleaning and preparing food. Alice was coming out to her place for dinner and Jane wanted everything to be perfectly planned.

It was three in the afternoon, now, and Alice was due to arrive as soon as her last client left the salon. Jane had steak from her freezer, thawed, salad and potatoes from her garden, and she knew Alice would never believe it, but she even had wine she made the year before from her own concord grape vines. She had a fruit dish of cantaloupe and strawberries from her garden and blackberries from the wooded area beyond her yard and along the road. Jane used just a bit of marijuana buds to make her special brownies to go with her homemade ice cream for desert. The bread was mixed up, rising and soon ready to bake. She looked around the farm house and everything looked perfect. The table was set; the charcoal coals were getting hot when she heard

Alice's Camaro pull into the yard. She ran down the back porch steps, she was so excited to see her.

"Nice wheels," Jane said. She greeted Alice with a kiss on the cheek as Alice got out of her car. Alice was wearing a short black skirt and low cut white blouse. The sight of her gave Jane a stirring feeling.

"Must say I've never had them called that before," smiled Alice as she leaned forward to kiss Jane on the lips. They both laughed.

"Good one," Jane said, her heart pounding with desire. She wanted to yank that top right off but refrained, "and yes, very nice indeed" she added.

"Later my dear," smiled Alice sliding her arm in Jane's and leading her into the house. "Do I smell a fire burning?"

"Yes, you do, and I was just about ready to the put the steaks on the grill." Jane headed to the refrigerator, "Everything is home grown here, the steaks come from the neighbor down the road who raises grass fed black Angus beef. I don't think you will be disappointed."

"What can I get you to drink?" Jane said holding up a wine glass. "You name it, and I just might have it."

"I don't doubt that, considering your lavish menu," smiled Alice, "how about a glass of the wine that you made last year, the one you were telling me about?" Alice said stepping into the kitchen to get closer to Jane. She suddenly wanted to be very near and touch her. She was falling in love with Jane, how could she not? Jane was irresistible and so lovely with her pretty green eyes and silky, smooth skin. Alice had to stop thinking about the wonderful sex they had and come back to reality, just for a while, at least, until they got dinner out of the way. She smiled to herself as she took her glass of wine and followed Jane out to her ivy covered lattice framed patio. The patio had beautiful inlaid brick flooring to the grill in the far corner, away from the house. Alice choose a comfortable looking wicker chair to sit in while watching Jane go inside to get the steaks.

"Is there anything I can do to help?" Alice offered after taking a sip of Jane's homemade wine. "This wine is delicious, by the way."

"Oh, I'll think of something for you to do later — after dinner." Jane turned to look Alice in the eyes and smiled walking over to kiss her on the lips, on her way to the back door.

"You promise?" said Alice wickedly. She almost suggested they skip dinner and go right for the sex, but she was hungry. She had worked straight through lunch so she could get off of work early to go to Jane's.

They enjoyed sipping "Jane's Wine" from her own personal label wine collection. Jane sat down on a wicker chair beside Alice, only getting up a couple of times to check the steaks, which were cooked to order, medium rare. The steaks turned out perfectly, the wine was robust and tart with a sweet after taste, the vegetables and fruit were to die for, as was the homemade ice cream. Before the sun set, Jane gave Alice the tour of the farm. They walked arm in arm, bodies touching, lips smiling and brains a little tipsy from drinking several glasses of wine, and taking a couple of hits of Jane's excellent marijuana.

Alice loved Jane's organic farm and was very interested in learning about how the garden was grown and the animals were fed. Returning to the patio they had another glass of wine; Alice had her back to the yard and did not see the streak across the night sky, but Jane did. A dang flying saucer. *Oh, so now those guys show up*, thought Jane. She was going to have to work out a contact plan with her alien friends, Moe, Larry and Curly. The craft zipped across the sky and made Jane smile. Alice would never believe this, Jane thought to herself, so why even mention it. "Please don't knock at my door tonight," Jane pleaded silently. Maybe they saw Alice's car and decided to visit another time. But Jane remembered what they had said, "We know everything Jane." So she just smiled and took another sip of wine and a hit from the pipe Alice passed her.

"What are you smiling at, my love?" Alice had turned to look into Jane's eyes.

"I'm thinking about taking you and this little bottle into the bedroom, what you think about that?"

"I'm thinking I love that idea," Alice said as she laughed at the tipsiness of both of them.

****

Jane woke up totally in love. They stayed in bed to till nearly ten, and when they finally looked to see what time it was, were surprised at how late it was.

"You have to get ready for your farmer's market sale today. Let me help you," Alice offered. Alice was becoming very comfortable with Jane and how she lived. She loved the naturalness of organic life. She had never been exposed to it before, being a city girl, and working in the corporate world since college. It was why she wanted to move to a small town. She was so glad she had spotted the for lease sign when her car broke down and she began her new life in Hank, Missouri. Anyway, it was destiny; there are no coincidences, everything happened for a reason. Alice knew that, now, as she held Jane in her arms and kissed her sweetly. They finally dragged themselves out of bed, got dressed and Alice helped Jane load up her truck and off they went to the farmer's market.

"I love this," Alice said as she finished propping up the price sign and helping Jane set up cartons of eggs. The chicken was in the glass cooler, and they laid out sweet corn, tomatoes, lettuce, cucumbers and several other vegetables and fruits to display for buyers. The evening was successful, the crowd was large that lovely evening and they sold everything. Alice handed out a few hair salon business cards and even booked a few appointments.

"This is great!" Alice was excited. "I love technology, I just set up several appointments with my smart phone." She had a busy salon week ahead of her and she was happy about that. She was just happy, period, since she met Jane.

"Oh, and I just accepted credit cards with this magical attachment to my smart phone," said Jane.

"Oh yes, I do that too, with mine," said Alice and they both laughed.

"Come on, I hear the band playing, want to get a beer and celebrate our successful market day?"

"I would love to!" Alice smiled as they walked arm in arm and bellied up to the bar. They bought a couple of beers, then found a small table and sat and listened to the small banjo-plucking, guitar-picking duo play a down home country sound.

"I love you."

"I love you, too."

****

Alice left Jane's early the next morning; she had to get to the salon for early appointments. Jane tended to her farm duties before heading out to go to work. On her way down her lane she spotted her three buddies, Moe, Larry, and Curly walking towards her from the spacecraft a few yards away. It was parked on the side of the harvested field in the grass.

"Hey, I've been looking for you guys," she greeted them and then added, "little unusual to see you during the day, isn't it? But, I am glad to see you. We have a couple of things to talk about."

"Well, we wanted to visit last evening but then we saw that your lady friend was visiting," mouthed Larry, before Moe elbowed him in the mid-section. Alice wanted to laugh, they were being very playful and very human-like this morning. She needed to get to work.

"I need a way to contact you guys."

"Oh there's an app for that," snickered Curly.

"No really."

"No really, there is an app for that," and Larry whips out his phone from god knows where. Jane saw no pocket on these little gray guys, with three long fingers, huge heads and almond shape bug eyes. She hoped they couldn't read her mind.

"We can read your mind. You dumb blonde," giggled Curly suddenly.

"Crap! My hair is not blonde!" Jane had to smile, what was she thinking, of course they could read her mind.

"Well, should be," whispered Curly, having a little fun.

"Back to business, I have to get to work."

"While you are at work, look up this man's profile, see what you can find on him; his name is Joe Breeze, here is his picture." Moe produced a file out of nowhere and handed it to Jane who sat in her convertible chatting with the guys standing next to her car, space craft saucer all shiny in the morning sun parked in the field across the ditch from them. What would the neighbors think Jane wondered?

"Here's that app," Curley said, as he showed his smart phone contact app to her.

"There really is an app!" exclaimed Jane, and she proceeded to find it at the app store and download it on her smartphone. Then she had a crazy thought.

"Hey can you guys control your space craft from your smartphone."

"Of course," smiled Larry who couldn't wait to show her as the craft suddenly lifted than tipped towards them in a greeting fashion. They really did not need an app on a smartphone but it was their way of bonding with Jane.

"I love technology!" was all that Jane could manage to say, but she realized they use their thoughts. The app was for show for her benefit.

"We must go now, there is a car approaching on the road," Curly said. Jane neither heard nor saw anything. But the threesome took a quick few steps to their craft, got in, beamed up and they were out of there in a flash, just as the car passed Jane's mailbox at the end of her lane. Jane was amazed.

Chapter Ten

"Good morning," smiled Captain Mike Moore, but then in a more strict voice, added, "you're late."

"Oh you say that every morning," Jane grinned.

"You're late every morning," the captain stated matter-of-factly, without a smile. He briefed her as to what happened over night which amounted to about nothing, then he took his hat off the rack as he headed toward the door. His shift was over and hers was only beginning.

"I thought he'd never leave." Jane smiled to herself, as she poured herself a cup of coffee, then sat down at the computer in the corner of the office. She logged into official files and did a file search on Joe Breeze. To her surprise, the information came up in a few minutes of search time. The police report stated the coroner declared his death a suicide with two shots to the back of the head. Jane thought that odd, how can you pull off a second round after the first self-inflicted shot? She read on; the report stated that Breeze was sick with cancer at the time of his death. Jane noticed that he had worked at MARTA and had filed a law suit with the company, suing them for unsafe working conditions. Whoever compiled this file made good notes. The case file was still open. Apparently someone thought his death suspicious.

Jane's detective mind kicked in when she saw that Joe Breeze had worked at the MARTA company; the same place that her ex-husband George worked. Jane wondered if George was still alive; he looked so deathly ill in the picture he left for her in the mailbox. She guessed George, himself, had sent the picture and the information. But she wondered, was someone forwarding his information to her for him and was he even aware that they were? Jane still wondered who the person was who delivered the first note and then the second envelope containing additional information about MARTA practices that she recently received?

She had both envelopes with the original papers hidden in her attic. She had shown the picture and the information to the aliens upon one of their visits. She had begged for their help and remembered what they had told her.

"We can only advise we cannot interfere."

"I beg your pardon," Jane was to the point. "Remember the escapee?"

"What about him?" Moe asked in his magical yet rather mechanical sounding voice.

"You put him back in jail as I recall."

"Oh no, we only appeared to him and he very quickly decided to go back to jail on his own," Curley stated.

"So, how did my truck get back into my barn?" asked Jane.

"He returned your truck, then ran down to the train tracks and hopped onto a slow moving train, into a boxcar with an open door," suggested Larry.

"After he saw your flying saucer?" Jane smiled.

And wasn't that interfering in a way? Jane was puzzled. What wasn't puzzling these days? But she let the matter drop for she was only too glad that her alien friends took care of the matter. The escapee that took her truck was a totally different matter than Joe Breeze and she had to look further into that mystery.

Alice had late appointments so Jane went directly home, after work, to tend to the animals and garden. When she pulled into her lane something felt oddly strange. She checked for mail and there wasn't any. Lately, she dreaded checking for mail, for fear of finding more information from George. She had not acted on any of the information George had given her regarding the test results or the information that she had found on Joe Breeze. She realized that being a deputy meant doing detective work too, but she had no idea how to go about this because she did not know who it was who had left her the information in her mail box. Jane wondered why this person wasn't going to the proper authorities directly, why drag her into this? She was being a little selfish and she knew it. But it seemed that just when her life was going smoothly and retirement so near, why ruffle any feathers? Jane felt that if she proceeded with her own personal investigation that her life may be threatened. Going up against a big corporation would be too risky. Jane parked in the driveway near the house and like always, got out and walked towards the back door. Something just did not feel right. There was a cold chill in the air as a gust of wind swept her hair across her eyes. She brushed her hair aside, and then she saw that the back door was open several inches as if she forgot to close it all the way, but she never forgot. In fact, she was famous for double checking everything two or three times before she left the house. Joyce and Pete would shake their heads watching her go through her crazy ritual every time they get ready to go horseback riding. Armed Deputy Sheriff or not, Jane was afraid, but knew that she had to go inside sooner or later.

She stepped up onto the back porch taking light steps, she quickly pulled open the screen door and peered inside through the open door. Her heart was pounding in her chest as she pulled out her service revolver quietly and slowly pushed opened the door a bit further. The kitchen was filled with late afternoon light casting shadows as evening was fast approaching. She thought she heard the creaking of the floor from inside. Oh she knew where that weak spot was on the kitchen floor and aimed her gun in the same direction. She flipped the kitchen light switch and her heart stopped at the sight. Not another damn escapee she thought. One she had not heard about? The man sat sitting at her kitchen table with his back to her. His hands were holding his head up. He looked up just as she came closer with the extended gun held out in front of her shaking slightly in her right hand. Wait, there was something familiar about this man.

"What the hell!" Jane was shocked when she looked at the beat up, bent over man sitting at the table and realized it was George. He looked a wreck, but not as bad as the picture she had found days earlier in her mailbox. Seated at the table in front of her, he at least had some color to his face, in the picture she thought that she could had been looking at a dead man.

"I'm sorry to just show up this way," George said, feeling her presence, looked up and then spoke in low, slow deliberate tones as if it hurt him to speak. He had looked up at Jane. How strangely she looked at him. How strange he must have appeared to her.

"How did you get in?" Jane asked.

"I used to live here remember," George said slowly, and in a voice not his own, looking up at Jane's surprised expression. She was filled with concern.

"Well, I could have changed the locks," she blatantly pointed out.

"I gambled that you didn't." He sounded sad. "I knocked, when I got here, and you were not at home so I used my key."

"You look awful George," Jane stated in a rather matter of fact, yet soft sympathetic tone.

"Believe it or not, I am a bit better," smiled George, sitting up taller now and with both hands smoothing his patchy gray hair back from his forehead. It was obvious to Jane that he was trying to convince her and himself that he was better.

"Can I get you something to eat? Water?"

"I'll take some water," George said weakly.

Jane went to the refrigerator for the water and brought back two bottles along with bread, a package of sliced ham, a knife and fork, mustard and a small jar of bread and butter pickles. She knew what George liked and put it all on the table and sat down across from him and began to make sandwiches. Napkins were already on the table and George took one to wipe the perspiration off his brow, then he got up and pitched it in the trash can and went to the sink to wash his hands and face then returned to sit in the chair across the table from Jane.

"Tell me what is going on, George," Jane spoke slowly but her heart was racing, she was eager to find out just what was going on.

"Was it you who left the picture and papers in my mailbox?" she asked.

"Yes, it was me, I decided that I could trust no one else," whispered George, "and as far as I know, no one knows about you."

"You weren't followed were you?" Jane said in a low voice looking him dead in the eyes thinking it then decided to say it. Worried, now, at what was to come of all this sneaking around and the hiding of documents.

"This whole whistle blowing stuff scares the hell out of me." Jane's eyes grew big.

"No, I don't think that I was followed," said George,

then added, "I am working part time now due to my illness. I have a sweep up, cleaning job now. They don't even see me. They pay no attention when I am cleaning up waste baskets and the like. But I overheard things and I have seen things."

"Are you keeping notes, taking pictures?" Jane asked with reluctant interest. She just wanted to coast along until retirement, not get tangled up in a whistle-blowing situation.

"Yes, I am taking notes and pictures with my cell phone," nodded George.

"The papers you gave to me showed all sorts of test information that I did not understand. Is there enough information and proof in those documents to stop what is happening at this plant?"

"I think that there is enough information there," explained George. "I just had to get them to another person, I do have other records in a safe deposit box near work, that is what the key was for that I gave you. Did you find the key?"

"Yes, I did," said Jane.

"That key needs to be kept in a safe place," George said with a dead serious tone.

"What can we possibly do, George?" Jane was frustrated but went on, "I mean these are very wealthy powerful people who control government and have laws changed so they can make and sell these toxic products for manufacturing and they end up on grocery store shelves and in restaurants. We can't go up against these people! They'll kill us!"

"Well, you are right, and I couldn't agree with you more, anyone who knows anything, or they feel are a threat, disappears or gets sick. Now you know why they always have an ad in the paper and always looking for new help." George explained.

"Yes, I know, I saw the ad that was posted in Hank's weekly paper. The same ad has been in Jefferson's daily paper."

Jane had finished making sandwiches for both of them and got out a big bag of chips. While eating a sandwich she began reading the label on the bread wrapper and then the potato chips bag.

"The bad ingredients are listed in several different ways aren't they, so it seems as to avoid detection."

"Yes it seems as soon as people catch on to one name, of a harmful ingredient, they just call the ingredient by something else or get a law passed where they do not even have to list the ingredients."

Jane fixed another sandwich for George, wondering the whole time that she was making it, just where the grain came from to make the bread she bought and where the meat came from. She began to feel uneasy about any groceries she bought and usually made sure that she bought labels stating organically grown and hoped she could even trust that. She realized that she was becoming very paranoid.

George ate the sandwich as they talked about how to proceed with the information that she had. She was soon to retire as deputy sheriff and was not an eager detective, or an investigating reporter, but she was determined to help George. George asked her to put the papers in the hiding place up in the loft. She said that she had done that right after she found the information in the mailbox. But now he wanted her to go up and recheck to make sure all the information was there. So she quickly finished her sandwich then headed to the loft steps in order to oblige him. She climbed up the loft steps at his encouragement to recheck and make sure all the stuff he gave her was still there. It was dusty up there in that space between the logs. The little bit of insulation that there was stuck to her clothes but she managed to pull out the box and open it. Everything she had put in the box was still there. She yelled down to George and reported as much. George never answered her. If he did she did not hear it. She looked over the edge of the loft and George was nowhere in sight. She had no idea how he got there in the first place, he just appeared and disappeared. At least with the aliens, Jane thought, I usually see a space craft come and go. She wasn't satisfied until she searched her barn and out building, apparently he just up and left. She heard the sound of the distance train whistle and wondered if he hopped the train. George had always been well aware of the train's schedule. He always said, close to their farm, was the best place to jump on or off of the train, if someone had to because of the curve it usually slowed down quite a bit near the farm. She wondered why he left without saying goodbye and she wondered when she would see him again. She worried about George and had suggested while he was there for him to stay with her but he had insisted upon going back to his place and continuing to work part time. He said that he wanted to be able to gather more proof and try to get more of the sick victims together.

****

Jane thought about George from time to time as she went about her days patrolling the county, going after burglars, stopping speeders and writing tickets for expired tags and driver licenses. She drove into the yards and got out and looked around for trespassers at the vacant farms long since abandoned by foreclosures. Jane always looked forward to the end of each day when she got to see Alice, the highlight of her day. She always felt so much better after she and Alice both got off work in the evenings, and they could spend time together. Jane had a hard time covering up her worries, and nothing got past Alice it seemed.

"Hey sweetie, have a tough day, you look a little down?" Alice was at the salon door, waiting to greet Jane as soon as she had seen her pull up in the car. Alice had just finished up with her last client.

"Hi honey, oh I suppose I did have a rough day, but I'm fine now," Jane said after she kissed Alice.

"You look fabulous," Alice smiled.

"I'm just glad to see you," Jane was very happy to see Alice as it seemed she was the only sane thing in her crazy world.

"Shall we go out to dinner or stay in this evening and order pizza?" asked Alice.

"Staying in sounds nice," Jane said as they climbed the steps to Alice's apartment. Jane grabbed a couple of beers from the refrigerator and waited for Alice to join her in the living room. She looked through the pictures and things Alice had on her shelves while she waited for her. She picked out the ones she thought were probably Alice's parents, siblings, nieces and nephews, then thought she must ask Alice more about her family. Somehow it seemed they always had so many things to talk about that they never really spoke of family, or of her husband who died. Jane was just wondering about Alice's husband when she came across a five by seven size picture of a man. For some reason he looked familiar, but then Jane thought he probably just had one of those all American kind of faces. Maybe he looks like someone she had seen on television. He looked familiar but Jane sure could not place it. She was deep in thought when Alice, after ordering pizza, came into the room. She had changed into comfortable sweats.

"Oh, you're looking at my roughneck family, hey?" Alice smiled as she seated herself on the couch next to where Jane had been sitting. But Jane still stood looking at the pictures on Alice's mantle. Alice took a sip from her beer, sitting back and putting her legs on the ottoman, then she sighed. Her legs and feet were tired from standing all day. One thing she thought that she should have thought about before becoming a hairdresser is that you are on your feet all day. But, tiring as it was, she enjoyed designing hairdos, being her own boss and running her own business. Still, she had to admit that at times trying to please and understand what a client wanted was admittedly more tiring than standing all day. All in all, though, things were going well, so she was happy that she was that busy that her legs and feet had reason to bother her.

"These are your parents?" Jane turned and asked after picking up an old faded black and white picture, in a black wooden frame.

"No, they are my grandparents, who raised me," answered Alice, then continued on to explain that her parents were killed when she was very young and that her father's parents, her grandparents raised her.

"They have long since passed away," Alice explained, sounding more tired than sad. That was a long time ago and she had put the past behind her.

"Is this your husband?" asked Jane, adding, but not really meaning it, just wanting to be nice, "he's handsome."

"Yes, that is Joe," answered Alice, just as the doorbell rang with the pizza delivery. Alice went to answer the door after Jane handed her some money. Jane then went to get each of them another beer, napkins and plates and headed to the coffee table and couch as Alice returned with a large pizza box. She sat down on the couch and opened the box. Immediately the amazing aromas permeated the room. They both were so hungry they each pulled out large triangular shaped slices of thin crust layered with pepperoni, onion with mushroom, ample tomato sauce, and dripping cheese. It was too hot to eat without burning the tip of their tongues. Neither of them could wait long enough for the pizza to cool properly and took huge bites. Then both made painful sounds, reached quickly for their beers, taking huge gulps to relieve the pain of their burning tips of their tongues. The relief would only be temporary. They looked at each other and laughed knowing what the other was thinking. Dumb move, but funny.

"This is my favorite," Alice smiled, meaning the pizza.

"You're my favorite, I'm glad you are here." Jane smiled and tenderly kissed Alice's cheek with her greasy lips.

"It's quiet and lonely at night here without you," Alice added, smiling at Jane, who was trying to stuff a huge hunk of pizza in her mouth now that it had cooled only a bit. Alice's life had taken such a huge turn after her husband got sick and died. Her husband Joe had gotten a job at MARTA, liked it, although he described the job as being risky, the pay was good and he was learning a lot, testing different chemicals he said. They both hated when he got transferred to South Dakota, then as soon as the opportunity arose, he transferred back to Springfield, Illinois. Alice knew the job was risky but thought risky meant possibly a temporary job, not risky as in health risk. Alice's mind was wandering; she was thinking about MARTA. She thought MARTA stood for Manufacturing and Research Technical Assistance but she wasn't sure.

"Hey, where did you go?" asked Jane, "You looked like your mind was a thousand miles away."

"Oh," smiled Alice, "just day dreaming, I guess, maybe a little tired; but, very glad that you are here."

"I am more than happy to be with you, Alice. I love you." Then she leaned over and gave Alice another kiss on the cheek with her pepperoni greased, cheesy mouth. Alice frowned just a bit and Jane burst out laughing almost choking herself and Alice laughed. Jane picked up her napkin and patted Alice's cheek.

"There, no more grease," laughed Jane wanting to kiss her again but she thought it was better to wait till they were finished eating. Alice laughed as if reading Jane's thoughts.

Yes, it was a match made in heaven alright. They finished the pizza and chitchatted a bit longer about some of Alice's picky hair clients and shared a few laughs. They had switched to drinking colas after they finished drinking the last two beers in the refrigerator. Jane absentmindedly picked up her empty can of soda thinking of getting up and getting them two more when something caught her eye and her breath caught in her throat.

"Well, I'll be damned!" exclaimed Jane, "interesting, where did you get this brand of cola, I've never heard of it before.

"Oh, I just quickly picked it up at the Quickmart liquor store down the street when I had a few minutes between clients this afternoon. What do you think of it?"

"Well I like it just fine," Jane said, "just never had it before." And probably never will again, she thought to herself, seeing that it came from the MARTA company, the place where George worked. Jane did not elaborate, but she had a bad feeling about MARTA; something about the place felt wrong, not only because George gave her all those papers to hang on to, but also how sick he was. Jane did not express her thoughts to Alice because it was just a hunch she had and she was only going according to her psychic intuition. Nevertheless, Jane just had a bad feeling about the whole MARTA business.

That night, Jane did not sleep well and she was trying not to toss and turn too much for fear of waking Alice who laid beside her quietly breathing long and steady breaths in a deep sleep. Jane laid silently thinking about George and MARTA. What ever could she do anyway, she was just a sheriff's deputy? She finally got up near dawn and left a note for Alice telling her she was heading to the farm to feed the animals. She kissed Alice on the cheek goodbye. It didn't take Jane long to get out of town and off the highway onto the county road. The rising sun was painting a rich golden light in the east. The dawn air was crisp and calm, she loved this time of day. She loved Alice Manning.

Jane was in deep thought as she drove home, she was about to turn into her lane which was now hidden by thick, tall corn stalks. Jane leased her farmland to several grain farmers who wanted additional acreage to farm. She knew they planted genetically modified seeds of corn, which was made into high fructose corn syrup. High Fructose corn syrup was added to sweeten most packaged products. She was happy though, realizing that most people were becoming aware of the ill effects of genetically modified organism products in feed for animals and foods for people. She was also learning that more and more people were becoming more fuel conscious and turned corn into ethanol gasoline and things made of plastics. She hoped one day soon that all her fields would be filled with organic crops, hoping too that the damaged soil could be rectified with organic minerals to recover from the toxic chemical damage. Slowly she was convincing her farm leasers to grow more and more organic crops. She got a third of the farmers profits and that money would come in handy for her retirement, but the money was not as important as one day seeing all organic crops grown in her fields. She owned the farm and the one hundred acres free and clear. The farm had been passed down to her from her parents, and passed down to them, from her dad's side of the family. Driving along the fields, she had thought that the corn looked tall but dry even though they had gotten lots of rain during the growing season. She noticed too that the ears of corn per stalk seemed to fewer than last year's crop. Jane was not a grain farmer herself per se; but through the years, over hearing her grandfather and father talk about farming, she could not help but learn and remember some of the farming techniques that she had learned. She remembered that when her dad farmed, he would rotate the crops each planting season between soy beans, wheat and corn. He did this to reduce the presence of weeds and insects, it took less cultivating, and no chemicals were needed. He used cow manure for fertilizer. They held back seeds for planting next season's crops. All this worked just fine until chemical companies wanted to sell chemicals and so docked the farmers at the grain elevators if there were any onions or weeds in their truck loads of grain. Her dad thought the whole idea of docking farmers was so they had to buy chemicals, to eliminate the weeds and onions that grew with the demand for non-rotating single crop corn fields. Big corporations wanted big scale farming and raised the prices on seed and machinery to squeeze out the small farmer so their land could be bought up by big corporate farms.

Looking out across the fields on her farm, Jane did not see any weeds, well no little ones, only a few giant thick ones that she could see. The crops rows were close and very thick. She remembered too when she was young how her father would cultivate the fields. A procedure that plowed out and removed the weeds between the rows of corn. Her dad would cultivate the fields several times as the crop grew, with an apparatus attached to his tractor, called a cultivator. This was done to root out and kill weeds. This could be done easily enough until the corn grew too tall to drive through the rows. But through the years the price for tractor fuel rose too, forcing farmers easily to switch to chemicals to control weeds and insects. Big corporate wanted to control what farmers grew and therefore what consumers bought in the big supermarkets. This caused problems for the neighborhood grocery and they started to disappear. The farmer who shared-cropped her land did not rotate crops because the demand was for corn. Jane had seen the farmer planting corn one day when she walked to her mailbox to get the mail. Striking up a conversation he had explained that they call it "no-till" farming now, with no plowing, just lightly disking and working up the fields before sowing the seeds. Chemicals take care of the weeds, Jane remembered him saying. She didn't like the sound of that. Chemicals. Why pour chemicals onto food people are going to eat.

"Chemicals," Jane said out loud not liking the sound of her voice saying the word. She vowed to re-read over those papers that George had given her to keep for him. Jane stopped after turning into her lane. She got out and walked around the back of her car to her mailbox. She held her breath as she slowly opened the mailbox lid and peeped inside. She wondered if she would find another gold envelope from George tucked inside. Her heart sank; there was no envelope, so then she wondered if he was too weak to put one together, or to deliver it to her or maybe he felt that he had gathered enough information. She hoped it was the latter. She continued to wonder as she closed the mailbox and turned to walk back to her car. She nearly jumped out of her skin at the sight before her.

"Shit!" Jane jumped and nearly dropped the town store sale ads that she was carrying.

The sudden appearance of her three alien friends:

Moe, Larry, and Curly, as they called themselves, she believed to mock humankind silliness. She could barely tell them apart, they looked so much alike but the one who called himself Moe was a little taller and always led the other two who trailed close behind. Always walking in line according to height: Moe first, then Larry and Curly being the shortest was always last. It was as if rank rose according to height. But she hoped she was wrong. She hoped that there was one place in the universe where living things were all created equal, shared, and looked out for one another—not like dog-eat-dog competitiveness on planet Earth.

"We no mean to frighten you," said Moe walking up to her car door as Jane was opening it to get in it. She had suddenly felt the need to sit down. The convertible top was down so Larry rested his long gray slender hand on the window sill of the car.

"What's up boys?" Jane finally managed to ask after catching her breath.

"Remember, as much as we would like to help humankind according to galactic promise, we cannot interfere,"reminded Larry in his squeaky mechanical voice, looking right at her. He was her height and eye level as she sat in the car. Was it her imagination or did she see him stretch as if trying to be taller than her?

"Yes, so?" As if Jane had not heard this before. They always say they cannot interfere with Earth's problems yet here they are telling her, more or less, what is going on.

"So we can't tell you what is up. But we know,"

smiled Curly standing behind Moe. Curly was always behind one of them, hiding in a shy way. Jane almost had to laugh at the thought, she was giving aliens human characteristics. That idea alone, with their startling appearance, was humorous to her, so she had to laugh off the outrageousness of what was happening to her.

"Think you better check on your chickens Jane," Larry suggested with a cock of his big round head, with big black almond shaped eyes staring at her. He spoke with a wispy sing song voice, as if mockingly admitting they knew something that she did not know.

"Not to interfere," Moe smacked Larry on the head with his long thin fingers and hand reprimanding Larry with a punch to the right cheek bone for speaking out of line.

"Err," sounded Larry in mocking Three Stooges behavior.

"Jesus." Jane couldn't help it. She just wanted to bust out laughing at the crazy comedic display. She wanted to tell the world about these characters. But why tell anyone, no one would believe her.

"We no Jesus," said Curly in a sharp tone.

"So what is with the chickens?" asked Jane becoming nervous, "did they get out through the fence?"

"Na, they're not going anywhere, they don't look so good." Said Curly with his head down, hands behind his back and swiping his foot back and forth in a semicircle in the dust of the lane.

"What?!" Jane asked she was not believing what she was hearing, or seeing for that matter.

"We no interfere," Moe reminded Curly this time, and slapped both Larry and Curly with one long sweep of his right long gray hand.

"Jesus," Jane repeated as she started the car engine and put the transmission into drive and sped away leaving the three stooges in a light cloud of dust. Looking in her rearview mirror she thought they reminded her of the Pillsbury dough boys dusted with flour. It appeared they were shaking themselves to shake the dust off. What? Did one of them give her the finger. They, had such long fingers, although only three, she could see it easily enough.

"Jesus," Jane blinked her eyes in disbelief.

Afraid of what she might find she drove up to the farm yard and drove her car directly up to the chicken house and got out of her car. As she walked around to the side and viewed the chicken pen she saw feathers lying everywhere and lethargic droopy headed chickens. They sat in silence, most of them appearing too weak to stand.

What is going on? Jane said to herself. She spied the chicken feed in their pans and as if a light bulb went on, she instantly thought of the new feed that she had bought. Her thoughts went back to that day when Pete and Jeff offered to carry the bags of feed into the barn from the truck. She counted back, that was over a month ago at least, she thought to herself and wondered if it was the feed. It had to be, nothing else has changed with the chickens but the feed that she was giving them. She immediately went over to the goat's pen to make sure that they were okay and they seemed to be fine. They had their own feed, it was different from the chickens. She had bought the goat's feed at least a year ago. She remembered that she stocked up when it was on sale. She had kept the receipt. Jane was becoming paranoid and began reading up on all the chemicals and seed companies and was disappointed with what she learned about MARTA. It appeared the feed from MARTA was made with genetically modified organisms of corn, herbicides and pesticides. She thought back and remembered that as soon as she opened one of the MARTA bags and began feeding it to the chickens, in over a week she thought something seemed odd about their behavior; they seemed lethargic. They lost weight, feathers were dropping to the ground as they tried to get up but were too weak. She separated the seemingly healthy ones from the very sick and dying chickens. They were in separate places now. Jane did not know what to do with the dead and dying ones. It was late and being exhausted and sick to her stomach she went to bed.

When Jane awoke the next morning she went out to the hen house with a shovel but found the ones that had been sick and dead were all gone, disappeared — all traces except for one she found in the weedy corner in the far end of the chicken lot. A deed gifted by the aliens, she figured. Wearing rubber gloves she stuffed the remaining corpse into a plastic bag, then wrapped it up good in freezer paper, labeled it chicken, with the date and placed it in her freezer in the basement. Then off to work she went, vowing not to mention any of this to Captain Mike.

****

"Good morning, Mike," Jane said as she rushed into the sheriff's office about one minute before her eight o'clock start time. Mike had just poured himself a cup of coffee out of the new coffee maker he had just purchased. Captain Mike Moore was a tall man, muscular, and quite intimidating to would-be-mischievous high school age youth and potential abusive husbands, in particular. Mike was one-half American Cherokee and one-half bulldog as reputation had it. He wore his hair shoulder length and usually tied back. He was rough on the young boys because he was a high school brat. He was rough on abusive husbands, because he watched his alcoholic father beat his mother. This went on until he grew big enough to whip his old man's ass, and throw him out of the house, after his father finally beat his mother enough to put her in the hospital. Mike had no patience for brats and drunken troublemakers.

"I guess it makes pretty good coffee. Want a cup?" Mike offered.

"I would love to have a cup, thank you," Jane just needed a minute to sit down at her desk and collect herself. What a morning! She was most disturbed about the bad feed she had bought for the chickens; and she had feared there was more of it out there and animals dying. It was the idea that the feed was apparently toxic, that bothered her.

"Hey, Mike, mind if I take off about thirty minutes

early this afternoon, I need to make a stop on my way home?" Jane was a little concerned that Captain Mike would throw a fit. He appeared to be in a good mood though this morning so she chanced it.

"Well considering you were about right on time this morning and nothing much is going on. Sure I don't care if you leave a few minutes early, just as long as nothing terribly major comes up by that time."

Jane was grateful.

Well, Jane wasn't planning on blowing the lid off of MARTA just yet so she figured it would be a calm day. Anyway she hoped so. She sat back and drank her coffee and looked over the file marked Joe Breeze again while Mike was busy talking on the phone to the county head office while filing out his monthly report.

Jane thought she should look over Joe Breeze's file another time, just in case she had missed something, anything that would help nail MARTA to the wall. It appeared that Joe Breeze worked for the company first in South Dakota then transferred to the plant near Springfield, Illinois within the last six months of his life. Joe had taken sick and had taken a sick leave disability before he even left South Dakota. Jane read the file until she had to go make her rounds and patrol the highway.

While driving one of her usual routes she realized that she wasn't all that far from the MARTA plant near Hank, where George, her ex-husband worked, and where apparently Joe Breeze was supposed to report too, but took sick leave instead. The plant was in her area of patrol in the far edge of the county, just off the beaten path and on private property. Jane had never even so much as driven past the plant before, and decided that maybe she should make this portion of the county a routine patrol route. She took the county road that led up to the plant. The guard at the gate booth, eyed her as she slowly drove by the entrance. Jane thought the guy looked a little guilty like he had something to hide. Of course, Jane reasoned that it could have been her imagination working overtime, which it has been, ever since George sent her his pitiful photo and those papers regarding the tests that he performed each day with different chemicals.

Alice called Jane and wondered if she was going to stop by her place after she got off of work. Jane did not go into detail, and only said she had to work on the chicken fence. Alice understood that Jane was on patrol and kept the conversation short. Jane saw that the ever vigilant looking guard watched intently as she spoke on her cell phone. Jane wondered if he thought that she might have been perhaps reporting something she thought was suspicious. Jane's intuition was on high alert as she drove and looked for anything suspicious or out of the ordinary. She had an eerie feeling; the place gave her the creeps. It looked dark and sinister and Jane could feel the negativity as she drove around the perimeter of the plant. Just as Jane was near the end of the circumference in her patrol car, she glanced in her rear view mirror, to see a huge industrial truck pull up close behind her. She decided to pull over because she wanted to see just what the truck was hauling. She signaled and abruptly pulled over to the shoulder of the narrow road. The huge truck narrowly missed the rear of her car as it swung around her. She got the license number from the rear plates. She saw that the truck was carrying large metal containers and barrels. As slow as the truck moved and the engine labored, Jane could easily speculate that the barrels were full. She wondered of what? An herbicide or a pesticide. She lowered her car window as the truck passed and noticed a strong ammonia odor. What did it matter what she saw, smelled or what her gut feeling told her, if working at the plant made people deathly ill it could not be proven that they got sick from working at the plant? She felt discouraged. She thought again: what if the chemical makeup of their products they were producing could cause deadly illness? Her hopes rose again with that thought. She was driving back to the office to get her truck when Alice called her cell phone again.

"Hi sweetie, I'm going to miss you this evening," Alice said feeling sad.

"Hi honey, I'm going to miss you too. Wish I could come over but I drove my pickup to work so I could go by the hardware store and pick up some fencing materials and work on the chicken yard fence." Jane neither had the time or the desire to go into great detail as to "why" she had to work on the chicken fence. She was anxious to get home and relocate the chicken pen to uncontaminated ground, and then make sure that if her goats got out of their pen they could not get into the contaminated chicken pen.

"Oh, okay I'll miss you," Alice sounded very sweet which made Jane really want to see her, but knew she had to tend to business at home.

Alice thought about driving out to the farm and helping, but thought she had better wait for an invitation from Jane first.

"Well, let me take this evening to get all the things done that I need to get done. I'll come by your place tomorrow evening, okay sweetie?" Jane said. Alice did not doubt her and even thought maybe there was some official police business going on that Jane couldn't talk about. She just had to trust her and she did, just like she always trusted Joe.

****

Alice was missing Jane, she was feeling a little down, today, and missing Joe, her husband. He had gotten sick so suddenly. He was always so healthy. He got sick right after he took that job at MARTA in South Dakota. Her thoughts than switched to her feelings for Jane. Alice loved Jane, but after Joe died she suddenly got gun shy about losing another partner. Would she be able to bare the heart ache if something happened to Jane? But she had already fallen for her and was in too deep to think about that now. She went up to her apartment after sweeping up the large pile of hair on the floor, cleaning combs and brushes, throwing a load of towels in the washer, checking her supplies closet inventory, and making sure her bottles of shampoo and conditioner at the shampoo bowl were all filled. She was happy that her business was doing well, that her orders for supplies seemed endless and ongoing. It was almost eight when she finally reheated leftover lasagna and ate it, sitting on the couch with her feet propped up, watching a cable news channel. She practically choked on a sip of Merlot when she heard the investigative reporter on new cable network NEWS say that a former employee of MARTA dying with lung cancer was suing MARTA for unsafe working conditions. A class action suit was forming according to the investigative reporter who spoke to the dying man's attorney. The attorney said solemnly that they were investigating further into not only the integrity of the plants which could also be poisoning nearby waterways with chemicals, but also doing a thorough investigation into the quality of ingredients of their feed and food products which are shipped all over the country.

"My god that is where Joe worked!" Alice said to herself and wished that this investigation would have been done way sooner before he took a job there. No wonder they paid so well, I'm sure they do have a hard time keeping good and healthy help for any period of time. Alice had a tough time falling asleep that night, and when she did she dreamed sweet comforting dreams of Jane.

****

Jane bought her fencing supplies and was grateful everything she needed was on sale and fit in the bed of her pickup. She wasn't wasting time and drove through a drive-through for a hamburger to eat on the way home. Going to fast food places was something she didn't normally do because of all the bad things she had heard about eating fast food. Funny, she never thought much about it, but as of recent developments and things she had learned, she realized why the food was so cheap. Jane forced her thoughts back to the task at hand and concentrated on driving. She wanted to get the fence work done today before it got dark. But, her mind drifted to manufactured food again, as she drove and munched on her rather tasteless burger and fries, she wondered about how the food she was eating was raised and grown. She knew that there were a lot of preservatives added, or so she had heard. But since the episode with her chickens, she wondered what the cattle were fed on those factory farms she heard so much about. She had heard, one time, that factory chickens were eating feed made up of chicken parts. Is that what they did with the ones that died? Were they selling this feed? And why did those chickens die before it was time to slaughter them? Did they slaughter sick beef and chickens? Jane was glad to see her lane to her house and make the turn into her lane so she could get home and get to work. The thoughts she was having were depressing her. Surely government oversight agencies were checking on all of these concerns that she and probably so many other folks had about the food they ate. That's why we have those protective agencies after all, she reasoned. Her mind was still a jumble of thoughts and questions as she opened her mail box and checked for mail. Well, okay, no mail this evening. I guess no news is good news, she reasoned, and shut the mail box. She climbed back into her truck to head the rest of the way home and get her work done. Well, no alien visitors this evening either. Then she smiled to herself, they probably flew over and noticed the pickup full of fencing and lumber and were afraid she would put them to work. And then her mind went on to thoughts of alien technology and how they could probably whip that fence into place in no time. As entertaining as her thoughts were, they were abruptly interrupted as she passed up her usual parking spot in the yard and drove back to the chicken house. To her surprise, she noticed a man in her yard and wondered who it was until she saw the saddled horse tied to a post. It was Jeff. Oh, perfect timing, Jeff. And then thought and wondered, gee you think it's' the aliens, oh, but they said due to galactic rule or whatever, that they could not interfere, hmm. She had waved at Jeff and saw that he was walking towards the chicken house now to where she had parked her truck.

"How'd you know that I was going to need some help this evening in order to get this project done before dark?" Jane said smiling at Jeff, who had an odd look on his face like he already knew why the chicken house and lot were empty and some chickens were fenced off into an adjacent lot. Jane explained to Jeff about the feed and how it killed some of the older egg laying hens. The Spring chickens for butchering were fine; they were in a separate fenced area and were fed different feed, the latter part Jane did not mention to Jeff.

"You're kidding?" Jeff said as if he didn't believe her.

"I want to secure the lot fence so that no other chickens or the goats can get in there." Jane explained, "I don't want them getting into the droppings."

"So tell me again what happened to your chickens? That sounded weird. When Pete and I unloaded the bags of feed from your truck that day I remarked to Pete how healthy your chickens looked."

"It was the chicken feed!" exclaimed Jane is a surprised and suspecting tone.

"You're kidding?" Jeff asked with raised eyebrows and a concerned look on his face.

"Yeah, the chicken feed from MARTA."

"What? What did you do with the dead chickens? Do you have before and after pictures?" Jeff asked, sounding slightly off beat Jane thought. He didn't express any concern for her chicken loss or her, but jumped right to a rather peculiar comment, Jane thought. He almost sounded like one of those investigative reporters she had seen on television news like more concerned about catching or maybe not catching the guilty party involved. Jane decided to proceed with caution after the odd remark that he made. To her it was like a red flag, a warning, of some sort, from what, she did not know, but her intuitive gut told her to take caution.

Jeff saw Jane's manner suddenly change and realized he should not have said what he said about the before and after pictures. He was going to have to be more careful. Jane had no idea but Jeff had been riding over through the fields several times a week to check on

Jane's chickens. He was curious as to see how they were doing after he saw that Jane had bought MARTA's chicken feed. He recognized the package easily enough having been a part of its design. Yes, Jeff was a big shot at MARTA. And right now he figured it was very wise of him not to mention that. The company, for which he owned many shares in, millions of dollars' worth, was being investigated and sued by some people who had worked there in the plant and had gotten sick. Jeff had sold off many shares in recent weeks collecting the cash and getting ready to flee before things got any worse at the company. So far the South Dakota plant was the only plant involved in the investigation and it was Jeff's job to see that the Hank, Missouri plant, which was supplying the surrounding area, did not get investigated or involved in the pending South Dakota plant investigation and law suit. Jeff thought he had better get Jane to talking about something else but she beat him to it.

"So, were you just taking a ride and decided to stop by this evening?" Jane was curious now; usually she just saw him with Joyce and Pete on their weekend morning rides. Jane had missed a couple of those mornings when she spent the night at Alice's. So it had been a while since she had seen Jeff, Joyce and Pete.

"Yeah, it was a nice evening and I had not seen you for a while so I decided to ride Roger over here," smiled Jeff. He always loved saying the name of his horse. For some reason the name fit the animal. He looked then to see Roger eating grass next to the garage near the house. "I was happy to find you home and glad that I ate dinner first, little did I know that I was headed for an evening of manual labor." He smiled watching Jane tack down fence wire as he held it in place. The project was going along nicely and it was clear that they would be finished soon. Jeff didn't have to ride Roger home in the dark.

"Yes, I've been staying at Alice's too and haven't been home all that much."

"Well, it's good to see you and it sounds like everything is going well with Alice."

In his heart Jeff was sorry to see Jane settled into a relationship, he did enjoy her company. But this situation with the chicken feed changed everything. Those bags of feed that Jane bought in town came from the Hank's MARTA plant. They were supposed to be shipped to the northwest area but someone got the orders mixed up. Jeff was not fond of knowing that bad feed was being sold. And his neck would be on the line. He thought of turning state's witness, but only for a second; he knew that would put his life in danger. He also knew that he could not sell off any more stock, he was being watched. And selling off stock was a sure sign of his knowing that the company may get bad press, investigated and likely put out of business. They were big, but unlike some global financial institutions, not too big to fail. Jeff had a Swiss bank account, and a place in Sweden, and he was planning on leaving the country. He had made up his mind weeks ago and was just getting things in order. Actually the ride this evening was to come and say goodbye to Jane. He was packed and had a private jet scheduled to take him out of the country. Jeff was sorry he could not set down roots in this area, he liked Joyce and Pete, and Jane and the other folks he had met in the small town of Hank. But, he knew he had to get out while the getting was good. Jeff was bailing on his mission for MARTA, which was to hide or destroy all evidence of the bad product that was sold in the Hank area. He was concerned with Jane's being a deputy sheriff and he had good reason to be concerned. He did not know that Jane was becoming quite the detective. She had locked up samples from the bags of feed. Before she cleaned out the chicken house and chicken yard. She saved the contaminated feces in large metal containers. She did not want to dispose of it anywhere on her farm or any location for that matter, the stuff was toxic and she didn't want it getting in the soil, or the water supplies, or in the air.

She was only a small independent farmer and felt sorry for the factory chicken farmers. She heard how many people had gotten caught up in the trickery of investing huge amounts of money in their chicken buildings and seen they had to keep on working for the companies in order to get chickens. She had read about the old style pyramid trickery to rope in non-suspecting farmers. In the beginning the heads of the company allowed the contracted farmers huge profits, then they talked the farmers into building another big chicken building with the profits that the farmer made. After the farmer borrowed more to build the second building, his bonus shares that he got at the beginning making him lots of money, were trimmed away. He was then trapped and in debt to the company because of the second building. He was forced into going along with whatever the chicken manufacturers demanded. Jane knew the details all too well because she had had to arrest a farmer in her county who got so distraught that he tried to kill the head of the company. The farmer was still in jail and no wrong doing was found for the head of the company. Jane was deep in thought about all of this as they worked on the fence.

"Hey, Earth to Jane!" smiled Jeff. "You certainly are an intense worker."

"Thank you so much for helping me," Jane was truly grateful. "I couldn't have finished this in one evening if you had not showed up." Jeff had been a big help digging fence post and stringing chicken wire.

"It was good visiting with you, even though you are a quiet worker," smiled Jeff, "how about we four get together this weekend one morning and ride?" Jeff's plan was to be long gone by the weekend. It was either leave or have to stick around and fulfill his mission for the company, which was to hide evidence of any wrong doing, even if it meant roughing up and threatening Jane.

Jane agreed to the weekend ride and then watched as Jeff mounted his horse and rode off across the field towards his place. She waved back when he turned to wave as if he knew she was watching him. Jane was watching him because she was thinking about what he had said about having before and after pictures. Jane thought that statement implicated him somehow. Why would that be the first thing that Jeff thought about, it certainly wasn't the first thing Jane thought about before she fed the feed to the chickens; who thinks of that? Jane remembered Joyce and Pete saying that they did not know much about Jeff. And even if you had before and after pictures it would take autopsies and lab tests to prove it was the feed. Jane got an idea; why not send a sample of that feed to the official county lab they used when determining evidence? She was surprised that she had not thought of it sooner. She then went to bed and slept restlessly all night and was actually glad when daylight brought the morning sun shining through the edges of her bedroom curtains.

Jane got up and checked on the remaining chickens and her goats. She made sure that they had plenty of feed and water. She checked on the goats in their pen and they appeared to be doing fine. They were excited to see her and came up to the fence begging to be petted. Jane reached through the wire to oblige each of them for a few minutes. Then she headed to the barn to get straw to wheelbarrow over to the goats building. When she got to the barn, it took a few minutes for her eyes to grow accustomed to the dim light in the barn. Jane thought something felt weird. Something was moved or gone she thought. And after her eyes adjusted and she could see better, she realized the six bags of chicken feed that Pete and Jeff unloaded for her, were no longer there. She knew that she didn't move them anywhere, so what was going on? It was unsettling to know that the bags were there the last time she was in the barn and now they were gone. To have them missing made her feel queasy in the pit of her stomach. It meant someone had been there in her barn and took the bags. Why? Whoever it was, did not want the feed there. Perhaps someone took the feed so it could not be tested and used for evidence regarding dying chickens or maybe even George's illness. She wondered how many others had gotten sick, animals or workers who worked in the feed plant. Jane wondered how big the batch of feed was that was bad; were there other farmers with sick animals? But whatever, the problem was big enough that someone or some people did not want any evidence lying around. She had called the feed store where she bought the feed and the manager said that he knew of no recalls, or of any other farmers having problems. Or did he just choose not to tell her the truth, she wondered. Or worse yet, was someone only out to get her? Why? She wondered if George getting sick and her chickens getting sick and dying could somehow be connected. Whoever took the bags full of feed she had stored in the barn had to be someone who knew she had the feed and did that person know it made the chickens sick? Jeff knew, he helped her with the fence. But that was just last night. Did he drive back over during the night and get the bags of feed? She tried to remember the last time she had been in the barn and seen those bags of feed. She could not quit remember; it had to be over a week or more. She had no reason to go to that corner of the barn until today when the goats needed straw or until her big feed containers near the chicken house needed refilling and that was usually every few days to a week. If Jeff suspected the feed to be bad and wanted to help her out and have it tested why didn't he say so? And what other reason could Jeff have to take the feed. It wasn't Alice, she never told her. Jane knew that she never told Alice about the effects of the bad feed on the chickens. George didn't know. The only people who knew she had bought the feed was the guy at the store where she bought it. Joyce, Pete and Jeff knew because they were at her house and saw the bags in the truck. Pete and Jeff unloaded the bags for her. Pete wouldn't have a reason, would he? Trying to make sense of it all, just made her more confused. She thought that maybe she could find more clues in the papers she had in the attic that she was keeping for George. She went up to the attic. The papers were still there, she paged through them again, but nothing stood out. The samples from each of the six chicken feed bags were there, too. So even though the bags were gone from the barn, she still had the small samples. Jane wanted to do all that she could to protect the information that George gave her. And as soon as George gave her the papers, she made copies and opened a safe deposit box, and notified her attorney, Ed Houston. They were the only two who had keys and could sign in for it.

Chapter Eleven

It was Friday morning and Jane had plans with Alice that evening as soon as she got off of work. She got up early and tended to the animals; they would be fine until she got home the next morning. She left a voice message with Pete and Joyce that she would not be horseback riding with them the next morning.

Before she stepped into the shower, Jane received a call from captain Mike Moore he sounded busy and was very formal.

"We have an apparent murder or suicide case this morning," he announced.

"Oh, what's going on?" Jane's adrenalin was flowing.

"A neighbor found a guy dead; he was shot in the head."

"Where?" Jane asked.

"Actually, out your way, so don't drive in, go directly there this morning to check this out. It's your case now,

I just promoted you to detective, since I can't get ahold of Sam," Mike mumbled. "Dumb bastard, he talked about retiring. Odd way to do it." Mike's voice returned to his official tone.

"Neighbors found a Mr. Jeff Holder shot in the head."

"What!" Jane could not believe what she was hearing. "I know him!" she added with stark shock and surprise in her voice. She couldn't believe what the captain was telling her.

"Yeah, neighbors Joyce and Pete Johnson rode over to his place; said they were going to go horseback riding with him. When he didn't answer the door, they peeped in the window, they said, and saw him lying on the floor. They thought maybe he passed out or had a heart attack. So they broke in, and when they got to him found that he was dead and called police."

Jane did not know what to think, but she had her suspicions, either he killed himself or was murdered she thought. Jane had a funny feeling about this.

"I'll get right over there." She hung up quickly and hurried to get dressed in street clothes. Odd way to get promoted she thought. The idea made her excited and nervous at the same time. She always wanted to be a detective but certainly not under these circumstances.

****

When Jane was ready she got in her car and turned out of her lane in the opposite direction to town, and drove down the county highway. She passed Joyce and Pete's lane, drove about another mile then turned left into Jeff Holder's lane and drove about a quarter mile up to his farm place. Immediately she saw flashing police car lights and several first responder vehicles parked in the yard near the house. She drove slowly up to the yard as to not stir up a lot of dust onto the people who were standing around the vehicles. She parked her car and walked up onto the porch slowly while listening to conversations around her. She wished Captain Mike would have contacted her sooner so she could have arrived at the scene with everyone else.

The highway patrol was there. They had put up the yellow crime scene tape and assisted the coroner. Something felt off about the whole scene; it was as if they were all in a hurry to declare it a suicide and get the body out of there. The coroner was about to give the signal to take the body away. She asked them to wait, and said that she was the detective on the case. Jane took a quick look around nodded at several of the officers she knew.

The coroner had declared Jeff's death a suicide yet it was obvious to Jane's untrained forensic eye that there were two bullet entry wounds near the lower back of his head. How does that happen when you commit suicide she wondered? How do you pull the trigger for the second shot? She quickly took a couple of zoomed in pictures of his wounds. She got enough of his face, included in the cell phone photos, to clearly see that it was a picture of Jeff Holder. She quickly put her cell phone back in her pocket, confident that no one saw her take the pictures. At this point she felt she could not trust anyone that was there. But as it was, they were all too busy writing reports and speaking to each other, they didn't pay much attention to her. Jane looked around and saw the revolver lying next to Jeff's right hand. Too close to his hand she thought. If he was standing there in the kitchen by the island and pulled the trigger, the gun would have dropped further away, she thought. Another thing—she knew Jeff was left handed. She just worked with him on putting up the fence. He used the hammer and wire cutters with his left hand. Her intuition told her that the gun was placed next to his right hand after he dropped to the floor.

Jane had a queasy feeling in her gut, suddenly her preretirement quiet mundane job wasn't so dull and routine anymore. This murder being declared a suicide made the situation much worse than she could imagine. It was most likely a MARTA coverup murder made to look like a suicide. Jane felt that she had to be extra careful. Any official, such as the coroner, could have been paid off. She saw packed luggage sitting near the door. Why would you pack suitcases then kill yourself? It was obvious to Jane that whoever killed him did not care if someone thought it was a murder, otherwise they would have been more careful and perhaps unpacked Jeff's bags. Jane's new found detective mind was going in every direction at this point. She was thinking of all the possible scenarios.

Jane did not know who to trust now; was the coroner in on it? He sure wanted to move the body right away. She argued with him but he would not listen. Jane did not know what to think, the gun that laid on the floor next to Jeff was a revolver not an automatic, she could see maybe a suicide with two shots if Jeff had used an automatic weapon. But this revolver had to be cocked.

She felt she still had to look at this case as if it were a murder case even though the coroner declared it a suicide. He was about it leave town, was it personal, business, or an escape attempt? She had to do more checking on Jeff Holder's professional and personal life and do it quietly. Jane thought to herself, what would she do with the information once she found out what was truly going on? Who could she turn to for help and justice for the death of Jeff Holder? Jane walked around the house looking for more evidence.

Things became more clear when she found Jeff's briefcase in his home office. She emptied it out on his desk and every note and paper that fell out had the MARTA's letterhead on it. Things were beginning to come together now for her. Jeff was involved with MARTA. She thought of Jeff asking her if she took before and after pictures of her chickens. She thought about how odd that sounded at the time. Now she knew why.

She headed out of the house and slipped into the barn, she waited a minute for her eyes to adjust from bright sunlight to the dark shadows of the barn. She walked a bit down the walkway between the stalls, past the storage bins and then she spotted the bags of feed with the MARTA label on them. Were these her bags that she had in her barn and that were missing? She counted and there were six bags stacked in the corner. She looked closer and saw the feed store tag where she had bought them. They had been opened, her bags were opened because she had taken samples from each of them.

She did not like where her train of thought was going and that was to MARTA. So Jeff worked for MARTA. Jane pulled her car around to the back of the barn where no one could see and slipped samples from each bag, marked it evidence" into her trunk along with the brief case and paper work she found in the office in the house. She had sales slips at home that proved the chicken feed she found in the barn came from the Hank store. And she had her samples at home. If MARTA had Jeff killed they certainly would stop at nothing to hide evidence, she thought.

Jane drove her car around to the front of the barn and back of the house to where all the cars were parked. She saw Joyce and Pete. They appeared to be in shock.

"Jane!" they both said in unison taking a step towards her. Joyce was dressed in her riding garb; Jane saw their horses tied to the wooden fence near the barn.

"It's a terrible thing," Jane said hugging them both.

"They said it's a suicide," Pete whispered as if he couldn't imagine Jeff doing such a thing. They stood and watched as the coroner's people place the corpse in the ambulance. Jane knew the routine: that it would be taken to the medical examiner's office for an autopsy to be performed.

"Are you both able to ride back to your place okay?" Jane asked.

"Yeah, sure we'll be okay," Pete said, "just a little

shook up. We just rode over to see if he wanted to go for a horseback ride with us… and then this."

They mounted their horses and waved to Jane as they slowly roe towards home.

****

"Hey, you didn't come by the salon this morning." Alice's messages sounded concerned. It was so unlike Jane to not call, but then a customer came into the salon and said that there was a suicide somewhere. Alice figured then that she would learn more about it from Jane whenever she found the time to call her. She went about work in her salon then.

Jane was knee deep in the investigation, there were ideas and leads that she had to tend to. She was not ready to share everything with her captain and just told him that she was still working on it. Jane called Alice after reporting to Captain Mike.

"Hi sweetie, sorry I couldn't get back to you sooner."

"Are you okay, I heard that there was a shooting or something?"

"Yes, an apparent suicide," Jane only gave her basic general explanation.

"So you'll be busy with that?"

"I'm afraid so," Jane admitted "the captain promoted me on the spot to detective."

"Oh my gosh, that's wonderful!"

"Well, I always played detective, or anyway the captain always accused me of playing detective. Guess

I get extra pay for it now. And don't have to wear my uniform anymore."

"Congratulations my love." Alice knew that Jane was working on over load so she offered to cook dinner at her house.

"How about when I get finished in the salon, I come out to your place, tend to your animals and garden and make dinner for you?"

"Oh that would be wonderful!" Jane was so happy that Alice was so understanding and she loved her for it.

Jane could not help but think that the papers George had given her might have something to do with Jeff's death. Call it being psychic, as she knew she was, call it intuition, she was allowing her higher subconscious self to lead her.

Jane had finished everything she could do in town and had driven back home. Jane's heart was light; she was so happy that Alice was driving out to the farm after she finished up with her salon client. Jane had a lot to do before evening. She climbed the steps to the loft then opened the hidden attic compartment off from the sleeping area. She sat cross legged on the floor with a cup of coffee and went through all of George's papers.

She remembered the first time that George had left papers in her mailbox. She remembered his visit. She remembered the aliens visiting right around the same time. They had said that she would need them. Just where have the aliens been, and George too, for that matter, where has he been? She did not know if he was alive or dead. She wished George would get in touch with her because she thought that she could use him as a witness; that is, if her suspicions were correct that Jeff was involved somehow with a MARTA cover up. Jane knew that it was either George or Jeff who came and got rid of the bad feed. She suspected that George was too weak to lift those fifty pound bags of feed, but Jeff certainly looked strong and healthy enough. Her mind was racing with suspicions and possibilities as she paged through George's papers.

She found something then, something written on the back of George's sick photo. He looked so awful she had turned it over as to not have to look into his eyes. Then she saw it, written in pencil. The name Alice and a phone number. It was scribbled at if someone was in a hurry. If Jane had not already known Alice's cell number she never would have recognized the name and number. The number was the number to Alice's cell phone.

"Jesus," Jane could not believe what she was seeing. She had sat for what seemed like hours trying to make sense of formula notes and chemistry illustration but It was all Greek to her. She was sure that it was proof of what George had been mixing together for MARTA. She would have to get it to a chemist. But the picture really threw her off. She began to second guess herself. Did she scribble Alice's name and number on the back of George's picture after she found it; it was possible. Then suddenly she felt a presence beside her. She looked up, startled.

"Did you ring?" asked Larry. "You called Jesus, so

figured that is our second name now, so we come. We can come visit, only when invited, such is galactic rule."

Jane was actually very happy to see their huge dark almond shaped eyes; they gave her comfort somehow. She felt that she could trust them.

"I am going to need your help."

"We know," smiled Curly "we are merely checking in, to let you know we are nearby if you need us."

"You guys are great," smiled Jane.

"We know!" they said in unison, "but we can't interfere."

"How can you help me, if you can't interfere, I just don't get that!"

"We are willing to step over the line if necessary; we will break galactic rules," and with that they left as quietly as they appeared.

Jane felt better now for some reason. She guessed just knowing that they were around helped. She heard a noise and thought that it was the spacecraft, it sounded like a gust of wind. It was Alice's car door shutting.

"Gosh, it is four o'clock already?" Jane said to herself, "where has the afternoon gone?" She had missed at least three hours of the day, was she concentrating that hard on those papers? She heard the back door open and quickly put the papers and photo back into the secret hiding place. Jane did not realize it but when she lost track of time, it was because the aliens were telepathically transporting information to her mind, unbeknownst to her. In space age technical terms, she was getting an intellectual software upgrade.

****

"Hello, sweetie?" Alice said looking for her.

Jane quickly laid on the loft bed, rolled around a bit to make it look like it was slept in then got up and looked over the wooden rail and tried to act like she had just awakened from a nap. She pretended she had been up there sleeping because she did not want Alice to know that she had been up there searching through George's secret papers. Jane did not want to drag Alice in on this mess.

"I'm up here," Jane reported stepping onto the wooden steps to come down "the sun was shining in so nice up here, so I laid down to rest, guess I fell asleep."

"Well you probably needed to sleep," Alice smiled, kissing Jane's sleepy cheek.

"I'm glad you're here," smiled Jane, hugging Alice and smelling Alice's perfume and feeling the silkiness of her cheek. She had missed her.

"Ready for the feeding tour?" Jane asked. Jane was going to show Alice her daily routine, so she could help her out with feeding her animals.

"Why don't you walk me through the barn so I learn where everything is stored."

Alice wasn't as familiar with feeding goats and chickens as she was with gardening. She had helped her grandmother in the garden when she was growing up but never tended to animals.

Jane showed her everything in the barn, the

animals, the garden, they picked fruit and vegetables that were ripened and ready for eating. They worked together at the sink preparing dinner. Jane had gotten steak out of the basement freezer earlier that morning to thaw, careful not to disturb the toxic specimens she had well wrapped and hidden in the back of the freezer.

When the potatoes were baking in the oven and after the salad had been made, Jane put the steaks on the grill. The steaks smelled so good, they couldn't wait to eat. They were getting giddy smelling the good smells, taking hits on Jane's home ground marijuana and drinking her homemade wine. They sat together on the wicker love seat on the patio next to the grill.

"Now this is the life" smiled Alice.

"I'm so glad that you think so," and Jane kissed Alice.

"I love you."

"Love you, too!"

They enjoyed a lovely dinner out on the patio. The night was pleasantly noisy with the rhythmic sounds of tree frogs, the night sky was filled with stars and sudden streak of flashing lights that Jane knew was a visit from Moe, Larry and Moe. She watched as they tipped the side of the spacecraft in a hello motion. She almost laughed out loud. Alice looked at her strangely. She nodded towards her weed pipe, Alice had just passed to her.

"Good stuff, don't you agree?" asked Jane.

"The best," smiled Alice.

They both laughed and sliced into their steaks.

"Perfect evening," Alice said glancing up at the stars.

"Perfect," Jane had to agree and leaned over and kissed Alice. She kissed Alice because she wanted to, but also so Alice would not see the space craft flashing by. Jane felt guilty for not telling Alice about the aliens right then. She wanted to, but her intuition told her now was not the time.

They wanted more of the stars, so later that evening they made love in the loft bed staring through the sky light.

"Oh, I forgot to tell you Joyce and Pete are coming over tomorrow morning for a horseback ride, they'll bring a couple of horses for us."

"Sounds wonderful," Alice said sounding very tired and they fell asleep in the warmth of each other's arms. They slept soundly through the night and were awakened at dawn by a knock on the door. They hurried to get their riding gear on. Jane quickly got downstairs first and let Joyce and Pete in. Jane had a cowboy hat and boots for Alice. Alice looked hot, Jane thought, and Alice had to agree that they both looked pretty darn hot.

"Would you like some coffee and a donut before we head out?" Jane offered.

"Just a little. How about coming over to our place for breakfast this morning after we ride?" Pete suggested, and Joyce nodded in agreement, her mouth full of donut.

It was Jane's turn to host breakfast, but when she stated so Pete and Joyce were so insistent, that she agreed to their plan. Jane figured it probably gave them something to think about other than the sight of finding Jeff's body. They still seemed a little frazzled. It had been a tough few days.

The morning was crisp and cool and the horses were ready to run. Jane kept an eye on Alice as she had not ridden in a while. She said she was a wee bit nervous, but Jane thought she did great.

Jane did not want to bring it up, but finally when the horses slowed down to a nice walk, towards the end of their ride, she asked Joyce and Pete how they were holding up. Jeff spoke for both of them, Joyce did not seem very talkative.

"Oh, it's hard to get that imagine out of your mind, but we are doing okay."

"I can't imagine Jeff doing something like that. I admit I did not know him that well, but I always thought he seemed on such an even keel, he appeared to have it all together. I know he lost his wife a while back. I had no idea that he had emotional issues," said Jane. She was surprised that neither Pete nor Joyce responded to her comment. But, they were walking up the steps to the porch now and she thought perhaps they were distracted with getting coffee on and breakfast made.

Alice looked at Jane then and wondered if Jane was doing a little detective work while she had Joyce and Pete's full attention. Alice had been looking forward to a leisurely cup of coffee but she had only taken a few sips and they had been ready to set out on their ride. Alice thought Joyce and Pete seemed rushed and in a hurry, for what was supposed to be a leisurely ride. She had only just met Joyce and Pete and wondered if they were always in such a rush. She would have liked to had ridden at a slower pace not being used to the horse Joyce and Pete brought along for her to ride.

They enjoyed a delicious bacon, mushroom, and cheese omelet on Pete and Joyce's lovely patio.

"So, I assume the police are investigating?" Pete wondered. Jane thought it rather odd for him to say that for a coroner's report stating Jeff's death had been a suicide.

"I'm investigating; I am the detective on the case." Jane was baiting the hook and she knew it. The more she thought about Joyce and Pete the more she wondered just how well Pete knew Jeff. Jane was trying to get information from Pete because earlier that day when she looked through George's things in the attic, she found enough information to spark an interest in Pete and Joyce. Just then Jane got a phone call from Captain Mike.

"Sorry, I have to take this," Jane excused herself, smiled briefly at Alice as if to ask "you okay?" She then stepped away from the table and walked to the far end of the patio and sat on a bench facing away from the breakfast table so they wouldn't hear.

"Jane?" Captain Mike asked.

"Yes, it's me."

"Got some information for you from a nameless informer. Seems Jeff was a whistle blower on MARTA so he had enemies there; we found out he had a plane waiting. Be careful. My informant suspects the people who found him dead were the ones who killed him. The gun was not registered to Jeff. They suspect he was murdered. They are keeping it quiet until they find out why the coroner did not rule it suspicious but called it a suicide. I wanted to warn you but I gotta go!" Captain Mike hung up.

Jane almost hyperventilated. Jane always suspected that it wasn't a suicide there is no possible way someone can shoot themselves in the head twice. She wasn't an expert, that was mere common sense. She sat there for a few moments pretending she was still on the phone. She sat with her elbows on the knees, head down resting her head on her left hand, while holding the phone up to her ear with her right hand slightly turned away from the three on the patio. She sensed Alice, Joyce and Pete in uncomfortable small talk as they kept one eye on her. Jane had to think fast on how she was going to handle the questions she knew she was about to receive from Joyce and Pete.

She wished Alice wasn't there; she didn't want to put her in danger. She wished she had her service revolver with her on her ankle holster. But mainly, Jane wished that Mike had not called her, suddenly she even suspected him to be in on it. She felt she was going crazy. Had she told Mike in the past that she went riding with her neighbors. She didn't remember ever mentioning it to him. Her intuition was sparking up again, she had a very uneasy feeling that the shit was about to hit the fan.

Suddenly she felt alone and shaken, but she knew she had to think fast. Who could she trust. She had a smart phone, why not hit the NEWS app and get the national NEWS cable station out there. The app allowed you to contact them directly and report any incident or news worthy story. Jane thought that if she got the NEWS people out there and had witnesses surrounding the house, she and Alice would be safe then, anyway she hoped. She pulled up the app which used the GPS on her smartphone, so she knew they would know her location. She typed: "Hank county detective holding suspected killers of MARTA man." She hit send.

"Hey Jane, your coffee is getting cold!" Pete yelled.

"I'm coming," Jane smiled big, trying to appear relaxed and not like she just called in the militia, twenty-first century style.

"So, what's going on?" asked Pete as Jane sat back down at the table. "Any big news on Jeff's case?"

"Well, as a matter of fact yes, they don't suspect it was suicide because of the double gunshot wounds and the gun was not registered to him." Jane was hoping her voice was not sounding as shaking as she felt. This was a potential life and death situation, she had to play it cool for her and Alice's sake.

"You mean the murderer had been in that house?" asked Alice nervously looking at all three of them. Pete and Joyce glanced at each other.

"Seems Jeff was a whistle blower for MARTA and had enemies," Jane pushed on, knowing that if Pete and Joyce were guilty of anything, this would stir up the flames. She was surprised when it was Alice who spoke rather than Pete.

"MARTA? That's where Joe worked in South Dakota!" Alice sounded angry, and went on, "I saw it on the news, yesterday morning, they're being sued!"

"Knowingly having toxic working environments and knowingly distributing toxic products and then trying to cover up animal and human sickness as a result," Jane added.

"What?" Alice sat with her mouth open. Pete and Joyce said nothing only looked at each other as if to ask each other, "how do we handle these two?" It was Alice who spoke next.

"My husband Joe, got deathly ill soon after working in MARTA's lab. He's dead."

Jane was just as surprised to hear this as Joyce and Pete. She knew Alice's husband died of an illness, but she had no idea he worked for MARTA.

"The South Dakota location was called, Manufacturers Analysts Research not MARTA which stands for Manufacturers Analyst Research Trans Associations," said Alice. Jane could not believe she and Alice had never had this conversation.

"I can't believe we have this in common. Maybe illness caused by corporations are more common than what we think." Jane couldn't believe what she was hearing and went on, "After we divorced, George went to work at MARTA. Then he got sick, for all I know he's dead." Jane suddenly remembered the papers hidden away in her attic and safe deposit box. If something did happen to her, her attorney, could get to them and MARTA would not get away with what they have done to animals, workers and consumers. Jane knew that she had to question Pete and Joyce further. They were not telling her everything. She wondered, was Pete a hit man for MARTA hired by them to go after whistleblowers. It had been at least thirty minutes since Jane had texted NEWS. She knew they have reporters stationed all over the country and the world. After she texted NEWS Jane thought to start her smart phone recorder. Her phone was in her jacket vest pocket; she was hoping it was recording their conversations.

"Pete tell me more. I know you did not know Jeff for a very long time. Did you know his wife? Was she with him when he moved in? Did she live here too before she got sick?" Jane looked directly into Pete's eyes hoping to see some hint that he was lying or telling the truth.

"She was with him when they moved in. They both worked at MARTA. She in the lab. I don't know what Jeff actually did at MARTA. I think he traveled a lot for them," Joyce said. Taking a breath she continued, "We would check on the house for him, when he traveled."

Pete suddenly gave Joyce a threatening glare as if she should not have said what she said. This made Jane think, that if they had a key, they had access, anytime. They could have sneaked in and waited for him then assassinated him. Did Pete kill Jeff, and Joyce didn't know it? Jane wanted to hear more.

"Where did you get the gun, Pete?" Jane blatantly asked she wanted to surprise him with her accusation.

Joyce and Alice looked startled. Pete almost answered her question then hesitated with apparent caution.

"What?"

"I think you killed Jeff," Jane said accusingly. She wanted to shake him up. She wanted him to make his move, because the three had their backs to the road and didn't hear nor see the approaching line of vehicles coming up the lane and through the field. Jane hoped to god it was not a hopeful illusion but that she was actually seeing what she thought she was seeing.

"Pete, say something!" Joyce commanded as if she had suspected her husband all along.

Suddenly Pete jumped up and pushed his chair away taking three steps back so they would all be in front of him and he could watch them all.

"Pete, what are you doing?" cried Joyce. "Where did you get that gun?" She knew she sounded scared. "What's going on?"

"I'm going to have to kill all three of you now, you are all potential witnesses against MARTA. My father began that company. He never knew he had a son until I faced him and demanded he will the corporation to me. When he died I took it over, it was mine. We were losing money and chemical companies offered us deals on questionable formulas. Yes, we had lab people that soon discovered what was going on, and they were getting sick and dying, and we just hired new ones. We paid them a handsome sum they could not refuse. The drug companies didn't care, they were making tons of money, when people got sick from our products. We paid the safety regulators handsomely so they would rule in our favor. We were all making money hand over fist. There is money to be made with illnesses. Sure, we discovered the feeds were bad, the food was bad, but by then we were getting kickbacks from the medical arena, and the insurance companies, who took in lots of premium dollars but bailed on pay outs. We controlled everything — profit and lives. We were about to rule the world and Jeff Holder, a simple ethical idiot caught on and was going to ruin it for us. We were going global and I couldn't let him stop us."

Joyce fainted. Alice began crying and Jane only hoped she was getting it all recorded on her smartphone. She hoped the approaching vehicles would park at a distance and walk quietly up to them so Pete wouldn't suspect anything. She was terribly afraid she and Alice would be killed and she desperately wanted a life with Alice. Then the worst happened.

"What's going on?" Pete turned slightly and saw the approaching vehicles, heard the now approaching helicopter although it was still in a distance. He panicked, cursed Jane and grabbed Alice, wringing his left arm around her neck as he held the gun in his right hand against her temple.

"Alice and I, are going to walk over to my car and drive out of here or she will die," Pete yelled in anger his face red, his hand shaking. Pete meant what he said and Jane knew he did. Her insides were shaking. Joyce was coming to, she moans slightly. Pete didn't hear it as he was beginning to lead Alice away from around the table towards his car. Jane was worried, if he took Alice and drove off, he would get away, but end up killing Alice. He was like a crazy man dragging her off, and Alice tried to free herself from his arms, his tight grip was choking her. She was crying and gasping for air.

"You son of a bitch!" Joyce cried. And before Joyce could say another word, Pete shot her, just like that, right in the forehead. He didn't even blink. Alice screamed.

"Jesus!" Jane cried at the horrid sight.

Pete held his grip around Alice's neck. She was crying from fear and the awful ringing in her ears from the gun firing right near her head.

"The next shot is for you, sister!" Pete threatened Alice. Suddenly Pete's eyes grew large, very large, there was a sight he had never seen before. It looked like a spacecraft.

"What the..." Pete said, frightened out of his wits. He took a step back dragging Alice with him his gun still pointed at her head. Just then a sharp blue laser streak flashed and stuck Pete right in the center his forehead. He screamed and dropped his gun, as he did he relaxed his hold on Alice. Pete fell to the ground dead. The spacecraft landed and its occupants unloaded, just as the NEWS vehicles were pulling up. It was all reported on live television on every cable station around the globe. The NEWS cable station went totally commercial-free to stay with the unfolding alien landing event. People cheered everywhere. It was like the messiah, everyone was promised, had arrived. The NEWS broadcasted live and in split screens to feature people all over the world cheering, as space crafts were landing in several countries at the same time. There was a steady camera on Hank, Missouri capturing the scene at the alien landing sight and the people's reaction.

"Alice, Alice, it's okay, they're friendly," Jane caught Alice as she was slipping to the ground next to Pete. Alice was reaching for the gun that fell out of Pete's hand.

"No, Alice, they're the good guys."

"What?" Alice turned towards Jane with the look on complete shock on her face.

Jane knew that she had to convince Alice and the NEWS reporters as soon as possible that Moe, Larry and Curly were friendly aliens. Would they ever believe her?

To be safe the NEWS crew only sent one reporter and one cameraman, to the patio where Jane and Alice stood and where Joyce and Pete's bodies laid. The three aliens stood with them ready to speak with reporters. The NEWS reporter and cameraman were happily amazed.

"Finally we get to meet some aliens," the cameraman said smiling, "we've seen your craft many times but officials of the other news stations and government authorities warned us not to report on what we saw. They told us we were crazy and demanded we not televise the footage that we have collected, so I hid it. My name is Frank, Jane," The reporter said, "I know who you are and I know Captain Mike."

"This is Moe, Larry and Curly," Jane said. Alice cried

and the cameraman, Frank, let out a wild sounding cheer as he recorded everything. This was history in the making. The truth finally revealed around the world.

"Finally! This is history! Glad to meet you, finally" Frank said to the aliens who nodded.

"How did you know to come help me," Jane asked Moe.

"You called us, Jane. Remember you said, "Jesus." We not your, what you call Jesus, but we know you say that when you need us to show up."

Frank proceeded to interview the aliens as the rest of the vehicle occupants moved slowly up towards them, acting as if they would scare them off if they moved too fast. Jane smiled. The world would now know that there are aliens from star constellations and other planets.

"Alice, I'm so sorry I did not tell you sooner about the aliens," Jane tried to explain to Alice as Alice stared at Jane in disbelief.

"We need to talk more," said Alice through her tears. She wasn't mad.

"We will, my love, we will," Jane said putting her arm around Alice and kissing her on the lips for all the world to see on NEWS; might as well come out right along with the aliens.

People were mad at officials and the government. How dare they hide the knowledge that there were aliens? The government excuse was that they did not want people to be frightened and feel threatened. This was not the case, people suspected aliens existed all along and wondered why the government ordered secrecy. What was there to hide anyway; that humans on Earth were not as advanced technologically as aliens were? Everyone figured that already, Earth had no vehicle that flashed and darted about as space crafts were seen to do. The aliens were a hit, and the NEWS now had three cameras on them, each recording individually from all angles; no one wanted to miss this piece of long overdue history. Frank, knew they existed and often got reports from airline pilots who could never speak of seeing UFO's for fear of losing their jobs, if they reported seeing them. Well, no more. Frank asked Larry to call in a few more friends and telepathically, in an instant the sky was filled with about fifty space crafts all on live television, Moe smiled a little smile on his slit of a mouth. Jane smiled when she saw Larry and Curly bow when everyone clapped.

"They are my friends," Jane announced proudly, as another NEWS reporter put a microphone near Larry's mouth he began to speak.

"Since we have the spotlight this day, we will take full advantage of it. We are aliens from the Pleiades, a seven-star system, main star being Alcyone, in the Taurus Constellation. We are in alliance with many galaxies and universes to protect this planet Earth from greedy evil human beings. We have taken a universal oath not to interfere, unless it becomes very necessary. We feel it is time to advise your leaders and heads of big greedy corporations that they are putting your planet in danger, because they only think of their billions they will make in profits. We are here to make you aware and protect you and the Earth from greedy wrong doers. Insecticides and herbicides added to genetically altered grain are toxic and pollute water, air and soil. This man Pete was trying to do away with witnesses and evidence. Greedy wrong doers who work with feed, food, insurance companies and the medical industries for huge profits at your health and monetary expense. Their whole agenda is huge profits for a small group while they control the population. Human beings are mere collateral damage to them, we are sorry to see this."

Larry was sad about the injustice of a handful of greedy people, whose wrong doings negatively affect all the populations around the world. He was sad but he wanted to cheer people up a bit and so he went on speaking at the microphone.

"But wait there's more," laughed Larry sounding like a guy in a commercial. He loved speaking into the microphone and he happily continued, "Besides our special appearance today, we are offering free spacecraft rides to our constellation. Yes, we wish to show you what it can be like here on planet Earth, a paradise, like Pleiades.

"You are missing out on so much because your leaders do not want us helping you, or them. You could be so much more advanced and stop these needless wars and learn to work together, teach and love one another and heal yourselves and your planet.

"Universal law states we are not to interfere and we have not, but when it comes to human beings destroying their own planet, we have to interfere. Because this would throw off the balance of the cosmos, as it did when they wrecked Mars out of war and greed. We can no longer stand by and watch." Larry said, "we have to interfere, before it is too late for your planet to recover."

People were cheering Larry and he took a bow. There were long lines forming for free space craft rides. The world was a joyous place.

Jane had given her smart phone to Frank, the NEWS reporter, and he and two other reporters listened and recorded her recording of what Pete had confessed. They placed it on the internet, they wanted to get the word out to the world. They were not taking any chances of courts, lawyers and judges getting paid off to protect these corporate crooks who cared nothing about human beings.

Everyone in the crowd cheered because they knew now that big banks and corporations, who were cahoots with government, would cease to exist. And that the aliens would aid in the healing of all the people on Earth and of the Earth itself. The aliens had to act now before the greedy destroyed planet Earth making billions of dollars to build space colonies on Mars. Somehow, the entitled super greedy thought that the Earth was theirs to use at their discretion. Their evil greed wrecked Mars, so they came to Earth, and now they were messing up Earth and trying to go back home to Mars. This was the evil greedy ones' desires as the good aliens knew it.

Jane looked up and saw Captain Mike walking across the yard with George, Jane's ex-husband. George looked ill but he appeared eager to speak with reporters. He told them how he had documents and proof of MARTA's wrong doing.

"Jane, I have a confession to make, and I need to make it now that I see George is here," said Alice.

"You know George?" asked Jane in total surprise.

"I met him at my husband's funeral; he knew Joe. I came to Hank to get this resolved. I knew MARTA was doing wrong. Anyway, I suspected it but I soon gave it up, not thinking I could get anywhere. You helped me Jane and I am most grateful."

"Yes, Jane, I know George, too," said Captain Mike. "George, came to me first, before he put the papers in your mailbox, Jane," Captain Mike said.

Jane could do nothing but stare at the three of them. She was stunned they all knew each other.

"These are new beginnings for spiritual beings on Earth as human beings, we are here to evolve, not wreck home planet, Earth," Moe said pushing Larry out of the way and wanting to speak at the microphone. Curly was busy showing people the spacecraft as they prepared to take people on rides to the Pleiades.

Jane and Alice stood hand in hand smiling at each other.

"This is so exciting!" said Alice smiling and hugging Jane.

"Moe, Larry, and Curly are not our real names, our names are too difficult for you to say or remember..." Jane heard Moe saying. "We are from the blue star constellation Pleiades; we are the good guys. Just as you have good and bad humans on Earth, there are good and not so good aliens throughout the universe.

"We can help you take care of the bad. The thing you have to remember is that greed and hate is out of style, love is in. We can help heal you and your planet. We can help you. In fact, being exposed on NEWS across the world has just changed everyone's consciousness and all unite in the betterment of mankind. You ask why now? Well, we had to wait until mankind was ready."

The airwaves were suddenly jammed; the corporate heads had killed the signal. They planned to call it an Arson Wells fictional broadcast for Halloween, which was a week away. Only a hand full of corporations owned all the media and broadcasting and newspapers. The buck could stop here Jane thought. She was worried that no one would learn the truth.

"Moe can you help us?" Jane asked.

"It is already in the process Jane, we are using our advanced technologies to override and fix this feeble shut down attempt. Your systems on Earth are antiqued. We have tried to advance your race, but your corporate slash government leaders do not want our help. Easier to control populations with old technologies. Except they forget just how powerful human minds are, they don't want you to know that either." Moe was correct, and in a second cell phones were working again NEWS was back on the air.

"Being so far advanced, is a reason your leaders have hidden us and you only get little amusing hints," smiled Moe, "we are the good aliens and want to help this planet and end the greedy poisoning by a few controlling groups. It's all about love, not money, the time of greed and domination for resources is over. The mindset has changed, the authoritarian age of dominance by demanding obedience is over. The authoritarian age of dominance by toxicity of foods and environment is over. The cleanup has begun."

Jane was suddenly stricken with fear, the nation's leaders, big shot corporate heads will never stand for this!

As if Larry read her mind, he put her at ease by explaining to her and the reporters that the only galactic rule was not to interfere, but we had to. "We are merely trying to change the hearts and minds of people to pride, integrity, honor, honesty, and love because your leaders allow themselves to be bought by big corporate lobbyists wanting to push their poisons onto the unknowing public. They think, so what if they get sick, then we'll sell insurance, medicine, medical services as band aids without cures. For to cure would mean pure organic foods, water, soils and air. The mentality is, big profits in treatments possible allowing or knowingly creating a sick environment then reap the monetary benefits. Most of humankind are aware of the facts but are caught up in the big profit spin, and feel helpless. We are not to interfere, but we have buzzed by warnings during wars and certainly while nuclear destruction is an apparent course, then we have to show your leaders, we are here. We are your conscience speaking, we are giving you a much needed voice."

The people in Washington and high places were not happy because people found out that they were lied to in regards to alien existence. People had trouble trusting the government before, they'll never trust them now. The government and large corporate heads are publicly, strongly persuaded to do their jobs and provide good paying jobs for people, stop wars for monetary profit.

Chapter Twelve

Two years after the aliens had shown themselves to the world on NEWS cable station, there were obvious positive changes to the world. People were happy and hopeful, they could easily see the positive changes that were taking place around the world. People were working together for the betterment of all life forms. As if a miracle had happened that day that the aliens showed themselves to the world, people united in harmony and love and began working together. Those in government and high commercial positions appeared to have a change of heart. More jobs and higher wages brought about more buying power and those in poverty were moving up into a more sustainable living environment. People were genuinely concerned about each other. The waterways were already clearing up. The air was cleaner, the soil was healing after years of toxic chemical abuse and able to grow pure seeds. Crops and food were abundant in every part of the globe. Large farms owned by corporations were sectioned and sold off to small organic farmers who sold locally and globally. Nations were trading their treasures; many middle eastern herbal techniques were brought back into the healing arena. More jobs, different jobs were being created and the pay was equal and abundant so consumers were able to afford to buy things now were demanding more merchandise and housing. Natural renewable energy was global. The Earth was blossoming in new found life, all natural.

Jane was a semi-retired detective. Her happiest times were spent tending to her animals and garden on her small farm and selling eggs, and produce, at the farmer's market and sharing those moments with Alice.

"Look Alice, the honey bees are back," Jane said and hugged Alice, as they sat on the back porch swing sipping homemade wine made from their vineyards. They sat close holding hands, looking out over their little piece of heaven, as they called it. Alice bought the building that housed her salon, she turned a portion of her upstairs apartment into an art studio and gallery. There she displayed her photography and paintings, in her spare time, when she wasn't being creative in her beauty salon. Between the salon and art sales, she kept very busy, as did Jane. They loved their lives in the small community of Hank, Missouri. Special moments were spent in the evenings on the cabin patio, gazing at the night stars, looking for their friends, Moe, Larry and Curly to do a fly by, tipping the edge of their saucer in greeting. Alice and Jane kept in touch with their friends, who came to visit frequently. Jane had been a big help to them. They knew they could contact her and she would not be afraid, because Jane, was a hybrid, she understood their ways. There were many hybrids on planet Earth, some knew that they were hybrids and some did not know; they were needed for when the aliens revealed themselves. The aliens warned that just as there were good and bad humans, there are good and bad aliens, and the Moe, Larry and Curley were some of the good ones and had human's backs. The aliens helped to protect Earth by warding off the offensive intruders who tried to disrupt the peaceful existence on Earth.

All the greedy, hateful terrorist types were sent back to Mars by the aliens. The planet Mars was once a popular destination for the super capitalist evil greedy types who had roamed the Earth, creating money and deliberating creating poverty, while they made billions to build spacecraft in order to return to their home planet, Mars. The evil and the greedy originated from Mars, but had ruined that planet to the point where it was no longer habitable, so then they came to planet Earth. On Earth, these Martians appeared as human beings and tormented the natives and took over their land and riches, as they did all over the world. They specifically designed markets and charged high prices so they could prosper while others could barely get by. The good aliens saw this and although they vowed not to interfere, they did when they had finally had enough and the planet was reaching the point of destruction. They sent all the evil greedy war mongers and thieves and for-profit crooks back to Mars where they belonged.

There is peace on Earth now. Love is the only way. There is no greed and no cheating people out of their livelihoods while creating riches for only a handful. The food is pure, and so health is excellent. There is no for-profit health care, only charitable health care. People are free to be creative and united in love. People are living to past one hundred twenty, and there is good and pure food for all because people raise much of their own foods on roof tops, gardens, and greenways through towns and cities. There are over eight billion inhabitants on planet Earth and everyone has enough food and space, and get along and work together now that the handful of super greedy evil spirits, who created religions, misery and poverty are back on Mars. The natural eco-system of Earth which was so miraculously designed has returned to its natural order. All the animals are in full natural cycles, as are the plants. All toxic chemicals that were used to poison people via medical so-called treatments are gone, as are the toxic chemicals that are ingrained in seeds to kill weeds. The air is clean because of solar, water and wind power. Now the Earth's natural north and south poles and energy fields transmit free power to all. This was as Nikola Tesla's had predicted, but was suppressed in the early nineteen-hundreds, just because a man who owned copper mines wanted to run electricity along copper wires for a fee to make himself rich.

The Earth is at a state that creation had intended it to be before the super greedy evil ones from Mars had descended here to rape and pillage the Earth's riches. They ruined it for themselves, because they were unwilling to share their wealth, therefore creating extreme poverty, which ruined the Earth's economy. Earth was near destruction and that is why the aliens found it necessary to interfere.

That day when all the world was tuned into the most popular global news network NEWS, the aliens came to Earth and showed themselves. People were not afraid; on the contrary, they rejoiced in hope. Hope for a brighter future where all those who inhabitant Earth is indeed created equal in life and love.

****

One evening, after the aliens, Moe, Larry and Curley did a flyby, they landed on the little farm, as Alice and Jane sat on the patio sipping wine. Moe, Larry and Curly came walking up the walk nodding their head, their big eyes looking all about. They were all smiles, well, as big a smile as their small little mouths would permit.

"Jane, we need weed," announced Moe, leading the three as they departed from their small craft they had parked under the yard light.

"I got the best weed this wonderful soil can produce," Jane said smiling proudly with Alice at her side.

The aliens joined them on their patio, settling in on

their lounge chairs that Jane got especially for their visits, which were becoming fairly regular.

"It's so good to see you fellows," smiled Jane.

"It's so good to see you, Jane and Alice," Curley said lighting up some fresh green buds in a water bowl pipe. The water gurgled as he inhaled slightly.

"See, weed is legal now. Inhabitants of Earth no longer need silly laws and rules when people are all loving and kind to each other effortlessly," smiled Curley.

"So, did you guys have something to do with people's sudden change of heart. I mean did you program us?"

"We turned the switch of 'love' on," Moe said. "Everyone has love in them, most everyone, except that handful of ugly greedy, hateful creatures from planet Mars, who were so intent to take from planet Earth."

"Now the inhabitants of Earth can get on with living on this wonderful rich planet, as it was meant to be, for all inhabitants to enjoy. You see every time someone on Earth said, "I wish those handful of bullies were not so horrible to us," we heard you. Your complaints were your prayers to us and so we came and we fixed the wrong that was on Earth. Everyone on Earth is happy now, rich and loved, helping others to learn and grow in wisdom and spirituality, as the universe intended from the start thousands of light years ago. We are your guardian angels that your religious people had often spoken of in the past hundreds of years, since your one called Jesus was introduced. The "Jesus," Jane spoke of so often. For your ancients who created religion knew, that we, what you call aliens, created your lifeforms on Earth as an extension of us. We created you as inhabitants to suit this wonderful planet Earth. We were most unhappy when a handful of greedy ones from Mars invaded Earth and hid us. Yes, we tried not to interfere and allowed the evil to go on as long as we could, hoping it would correct itself. But it did not, so we had to interfere and get things right after a few hundred of the greedy, wealthiest, and most powerful, came close to destroying Earth.

"We are most grateful," Alice said taking a hit from the pipe and passing it.

"So, I have a question," Jane said after thinking for a minute. "You, had me meet Alice didn't you?"

"Yes, we did do that," Curley replied.

"For a happy, loved messenger is a good messenger. Everyone deserves to be loved and you both lost spouses due to these horrible chemicals that this company was making," said Larry.

Jane bowed her head in memory of George, who lost his battle with cancer six months after she last saw him at the alien event. The data he collected was displayed in a memorial, as a reminder, of an oligarchy evil that once existed.

With grass roots efforts and the help of the aliens, people became aware of the plot to thin populations through illness: The evil powerful ones thought there were too many people on Earth so made billions in profits when people got sick. Treatments and drugs were not meant to cure, but designed for life long medicinal use. We all know now that they, the chemical companies, increased the occurrences of illness by brainwashing gullible humans with commercials that were televised with the sound ramped up, so there was no escaping the directed message. The Pleiadians had warned humans not to use the computer or to watch and listen to television. They did not want people brainwashed by the greedy.

"We are most grateful for your interference," Alice told the aliens with tears in her eyes. "I am sure that I speak for all humankind when I say that we can never repay you."

"Oh, you have repaid us many times over for making Earth such a beautiful natural wonderful place as it was intended to be."

"So, what are you guys up to now that you have saved us and the planet?"

"Oh, there are other places in the universe like planet Earth was, full of greedy and bad people," smiled Moe. "We are on a quest to help them too.

"The Earth is meant for all to be happy not just a handful of mean greedy people," said Curley.

"Before we came, people had to be born and be reborn to in order to learn life lessons because of the few, but mighty, negative creatures on Earth. Now those here are free to love and live hundreds of years if they wish. In the past, the offspring of Earth were born pure and innocent, soaking up adult actions and behaviors like a sponge. They got here and lived in humans' influence and their characters deteriorated rather than excelled.

It is why we came up with the idea of hybrids—aliens uniting with human beings. Your species was not evolving fast enough to save the planet from greedy destruction, so we had to interfere, in order to save you, mankind and your home. We are here for you always," smiled Moe. "We hope this makes sense to you."

"Oh, this makes wonderful sense to us," Jane said looking into Alice's eyes as she spoke. "We are most grateful for the caring love that you have brought us, to everyone, the whole planet. For love is the answer isn't it?"

"Oh, yes, you had hints when spiritual people would say—talk to animals, talk to plants for they understand and they feel; they take on the feeling of their surroundings," Curley grinned and took another hit from the water pipe.

"That is why your animals and plants are so healthy and good for you. You are all 'one' now as it should be."

"Is this heaven?" asked Alice.

"Yes, this is what your silly, selfish religious leaders promised you, only for their own gains," said Moe "but as you can see, we delivered the real goods, as you would say, didn't we?"

"Yes, you did," smiled Jane.

"Once more the positive love vibrations you inhabitants on Earth put out, rises up to the universe and the whole universe benefits. Did you know that those greedy ones who went to Mars are more like you here on Earth now?"

"No?"

"Oh yes, they cannot escape the positive love vibrations that habitants of Earth propel out into the universe. They are becoming nice people, isn't that a wonderful thing?"

"That is a wonderful thing!"

"Love produces love," smiled Curley.

And it was a most wonderful time all over on planet Earth and in Hank County Missouri, where neighbors helped neighbors and life was love.

About the Author

This is Dianne Zimmerman's second novel. Her first is "Emma's Run" published by BookCrafters in 2013. Dianne lives in St. Louis and spends her time enjoying writing, photography, drawing, running, hiking and road trips.